HAUNTED BORDER

HAUNTED BORDER

PATRICK DEAREN

THORNDIKE PRESS
A part of Gale, a Cengage Company

LIBRARY OF CONGRESS CIP DATA ON FILE.
CATALOGUING IN PUBLICATION FOR THIS BOOK
IS AVAILABLE FROM THE LIBRARY OF CONGRESS.

ISBN-13: 978-1-4328-7640-1 (hardcover alk. paper)

Published in 2021 by arrangement with Patrick Dearen

Printed in Mexico
Print Number: 01   Print Year: 2021

To Buddy Kinney
This one's for you, Bright Eyes.

CHAPTER 1

He captured her in his sights, and his finger closed on the trigger.

"Shoot her!"

Down the shining barrel of his Sharp's carbine, sixteen-year-old Jake Graves could see the front sight sway against blue calico. He could feel the walnut stock in his cheek as the butt plate pushed against his shoulder. He was strangely aware of the stock's forward end in his supporting left hand, a position that allowed him an unburdened grip behind the breech lever and cocked hammer. But no sensation dominated like the trigger's smooth curvature against his finger.

"You got to shoot her!"

A thousand times, Jake had shouldered the carbine and looked down the twenty-two-inch barrel, but never had seven pounds of wood trimmed with brass seemed as heavy as it did on this Christmas morning.

With a mere twitch, everything would spring into motion: The hammer would snap forward, the muzzle would flash fire, and a .52-caliber slug would explode between the calico-draped shoulders of his red-haired sister.

Maybe it was something that had to be done, even to a fourteen-year-old, but the trigger stayed frozen, Jake's forefinger refusing to obey.

"For God's sake, do it! Do it!"

From beside him on the porch of their homestead in the live oak country of Mason County, Texas, his widowed mother continued to plead, and her cries followed Jake across forty-seven years to this Christmas dawn of 1917 at Cross C headquarters in the Chihuahuan Desert of far West Texas.

He sat on a mesquite woodpile on the hard-packed grounds near the main residence, an L-shaped adobe structure under Capote ridge's low north end. The lofty roof hid the bare ridge's higher summits, a dozen bony knobs rising progressively with their southward trend, but past the corner post of the covered porch he could see Capote's two foothill cones side by side against the glowing east sky.

Jake twisted the bottom of his tin cup in his palm. The warmth felt good on this chilly morning, and the coffee's aroma should have been inviting. But all Jake wanted to do was stare at that pre-sunrise sky, its red bands as stark as his sister's red hair had been against calico.

She was there, all right, a haunting presence in the dawn. For decades, as Jake had cowboyed and flashed a Ranger's badge and, for the past few years, ridden the nearby border as a U.S. Customs mounted inspector, he had sometimes managed to submerge the memories. But now, awakening aimless on his first day of forced retirement, he felt troubled as he hadn't since he had fled Mason County at age seventeen.

If this was the way the rest of Jake's life was to be, he wasn't sure he cared to live it.

At least he would spend Christmas with his wife Annie, and their grown daughter, Drucilla, something that his law enforcement duties had not always let him do. Away to the north-northwest at Vieja Pass barely twenty-four hours ago, he had handed over his customs badge and struck out on horseback to meet them here at Cross C headquarters, a hard day's ride through the high-desert valley below the Rim. Annie had arrived a couple of days before, courtesy of a standing invitation from her sister and brother-in-law, who owned the Cross C's.

They were in Arizona for the holiday, but their daughter had stayed behind with Drucilla — or "Dru," as Jake called her — at Marfa, thirty-five miles east of headquarters.

Dru's arrival at the ranch had been delayed by her clerking duties at the mercantile store in Marfa, a town on the Southern Pacific where she still lived with Annie — and with Jake when he was around. If Dru boarded the afternoon train to Valentine as scheduled, she and her cousin could make the ride on to the ranch in time for Christmas supper. When Jake had learned of the plans during his last stay in Marfa, he had resisted the idea of the girls traveling alone, but Colonel George T. Langhorne at Camp Marfa had assured him that the road between Valentine and the Cross C's would be safe.

Now if Jake could only escape the memories of his sister so he could enjoy the coming celebration.

"Jake."

He turned to see Annie approach from the porch, a breeze whipping her dress. She was almost as old as Jake, but the years had been kind to her. She had gained weight, all right, and maybe the wrinkles at her eyes and gray in her auburn hair wouldn't have appealed to a younger man. But to him she was just as pretty as when he had stood weak-kneed beside her and exchanged vows thirty-three years ago.

"Lupe fixes a fine cup of coffee, Annie," Jake said, lifting his cup. "Better have you some."

"I need to go help her cook, but I wanted to catch you by yourself. You and Nub spent the entire evening talking about Villa and Carranza."

"Them two keep the whole border in flames. Wish they'd stay in Mexico to settle their differences."

"So what do you think of Nub?" Annie asked, stopping before him.

Jake glanced past her at the adobe wall that gave the house its L shape. Nub DeJarnett, the thirty-seven-year-old foreman, lived in this room addition, which was attached to the main residence but had no access other than an outside door. Jake guessed it was a way for the owners to justify allowing someone like Nub to live under the same roof with them without really doing so. Whites might work side by side with swarthy ranch hands, but it was unheard of to live together.

"He's all right, I guess," Jake allowed. "Long as he keeps his place, anyway."

Even in the muted light, Jake could see Annie's shoulders drop.

"Nub comes from a fine family," she said. "Don't you think so, darlin'?"

"I guess."

"What is it they call their ranch in the mountains above Fort Davis? Singing Waters? Wasn't Nub's father in the same Ranger company you were, back in the '80s?"

"No, Sam DeJarnett was in A Company. Well, he was before he took up with that Mescalero squaw when Nub was just a papoose. Don't see how a white man like Sam could've done it, not after her people killed his first wife."

"I think Nub's mother was stolen from the Mexicans when she was little," said Annie. "So he's just half Indian."

Jake stared at her; he knew her well enough to realize that she was dancing around something. "So what's this got to do with anything, whether somebody's part Indian or whole?"

"It doesn't make all that much difference to me, Jake. But I think it still does to you."

"You mean my sister," he said, sinking inside. "It show that much?"

"It always shows. It was worse during the night, all you were saying in your sleep. I guess you were reliving things."

"It's Christmas. It's always worse at Christmas."

With a deep sigh, Annie eased down beside him on the woodpile. She reached for his free hand, and Jake met hers halfway and felt a tremble.

"Want to tell me what's eatin' you?" he asked.

"It's Drucilla and Nub."

Jake straightened. "What about Dru and Nub?"

"They're sweet on each other. I didn't know about it myself till the other day."

Jake slipped out of Annie's grasp and rose. "No. You must've got it wrong. Dru's got more sense than that."

Annie stood with him. "She told me herself. They want to get married. She was worried how you'd take it."

"Married, hell!"

Jake's temples began to pound. He turned to the daybreak horizon, remembering again all that had happened in Mason County.

"If he's so much as . . ." Jake breathed sharply. "What's the matter with her? I'm settlin' this right now."

He spun on his heel, determined to drag Nub out of his room, but Annie's grasp on his arm stopped him.

"Don't you dare!" she exclaimed. "It's Christmas! Don't you dare!"

"Turn loose of me, woman. This is between him and me."

"Drucilla's twenty-three years old. Something this personal, she deserves to make her own decision, mistake or not."

"No damned Indian's marryin' our daughter. Mexican either."

"It's not Nub's fault what happened to your sister. It's not his fault they . . ."

Jake didn't need it spelled out, and for a moment he was back in Mason County and standing over a lonely grave.

"Besides," added Annie, "Nub's smart and dependable and a good foreman. You said so yourself."

"Yeah. A good *foreman*. But Dru deserves somebody better, somebody . . ."

"White," she finished for him. "Jake, I know the troubles they'd face, not to mention how hard it'd be on the children. That's just the way you and me and everybody else around here were raised. But if she and Nub love each other —"

"Love ain't enough. I loved my sister, and it wasn't enough."

Annie wrapped him in her arms, and her voice began to quiver. "I know you just want the best for our little girl. I know that, but she's all grown up, and we've got to let her make her own way. Papa wasn't any too keen on *you* at first, if you'll recall. I know you haven't forgotten what he said when he finally accepted you as his son-in-law."

Jake remembered the old sorehead's exact apology: *I always thought my daughter had to bring home a prince. But I changed my mind.*

Jake didn't think anything could make him chuckle, but the memory almost did.

"I'm going in and helping Lupe," said Annie. She had said her piece, and she wasn't one to drag things out.

But as she withdrew her arms, Jake glanced at Nub's room again, and Annie must have noticed.

Her jaw tightened as only hers could. "Don't you forget what I told you, Jake Graves. It's Christmas, and don't you forget!"

She walked away, and although Jake gave Nub's door a hard stare, he didn't move an inch toward it. Over the years, he had faced plenty of troublesome men down the barrel of a firearm without blinking, but Annie was another matter. For someone five foot nothing, she could be a powerful presence, and Jake knew better than to cross her.

Maybe it was because he loved and respected her.

Sitting on the woodpile again, he picked at his thick, gray mustache and sulked. He sulked even more as Nub exited his room and started for the porch outside the main residence. He was dressed much as Jake — sweat-stained cowboy hat, well-worn coat, leather vest, duck trousers with legs stuffed inside high-topped boots — but his features set him apart. In good lighting, Jake would have been able to see the rounded face and coppery complexion, the drooping nose and pronounced cheekbones.

Nub's was the face of an Indian. A *damned* Indian.

Jake watched him mount the residence porch and stop outside the closed door. In the chill of this winter morning, he would lean against a support post, dig out the makings, and smoke a cigarette or two while he waited for Lupe to bring his breakfast.

How the hell did Nub know his place when it came to taking his meals, and yet violate every rule of propriety with Dru?

As Jake's anger built, he knew there was only one way to keep himself from marching over and confronting Nub — he turned away, his back to the impending sunrise.

On a spread as remote as the Cross C's, headquarters took on the nature of a small settlement, and ahead and to the left, Jake could see the dark window of the absent postmaster's modest house. From a mud-plastered *jacal* just beyond, young Alfonso had started for the adobe pens and barn, where he would tend the saddle horses and milk the Jersey cow. Farther west, almost two hundred yards from where Jake sat, stood the Capote Store and Post Office. Set against the backdrop of the 700-foot hills of the Rim three miles away, the mercantile establishment consisted of two attached adobe buildings with high, A-shaped roofs.

Beyond the store came sudden movement. It was there among the big yucca, a wedge-like shadow growing larger by the moment. There was sound with it, a rising rumble that reminded Jake of the earthquake from the previous spring, and he watched as half of the shadow veered left and the other half right.

What in the hell . . .

Jake spilled his coffee down his trouser leg as he burst to his feet.

Mexicans!

There must have been forty of the riders starting to surround headquarters, and whether they were Villistas or Carrancistas or outright bandits, the threat was all the same. For several years up and down the Rio Grande, good people had died, caught up in a conflict that should have had no bearing on this side of the river. But the opposing armies of Mexico president Venustiano Carranza and the revolutionary Pancho Villa needed horses and provisions, and American ranches were all too tempting. The war had also bred deserters and malcontents, devils who had allegiance to no one but themselves and plundered where they would.

The U.S. Army's Eighth Cavalry and Thirty-Seventh Infantry, operating out of Camp Marfa, had done their best to make things safe. But images of four dead Americans in last year's raid at Glenn Springs, and another eighteen in the wake of an attack on Columbus in New Mexico, burned in Jake's mind as he bolted for the house with a cry.

"Get a gun!"

Nub turned so quickly that the porch post clipped his hat brim. "What?"

"Bandits! They's all around!"

Nub whirled left and right. "How many?"

"Too many! Got to fight 'em off!"

Nub ran for his room, his hat still askew, and Jake strangely wondered what it was like for an Indian to be the victim of a surprise attack instead of perpetrating it. Springing to the porch, Jake called Annie's name and burst through the door into the warmth of the kitchen.

"Bandits are on us!"

Annie's back was to him as she kneaded dough at a counter across the room, while the cook Lupe stoked a woodburning cookstove on the right. They spun at the same time, Annie with a flour-smudged face and apron and the heavyset Mexican woman paling for another reason.

"Get down!" Jake yelled. "Watch out for the windows!"

Always before, mesquite coals had given off a pleasant aroma, but as Jake ignored Annie's questions and rushed past her and through a doorway, the smell seemed to irritate his stomach. Annie's frantic voice followed him across one unpretentious bedroom and into another on the far right, where the two of them had slept.

Leaned against the mud-brick wall between the iron bedstead and a back window was Jake's 1894 Model Marlin, a lever-action carbine with nine cartridges in its underslung tube magazine. It had served him well as a customs mounted inspector, and he seized it and a nearby bandolier bulging with .44 Special rounds. Against the rising sun through the window, he saw a rider flash by at a distance of eighty or ninety yards, and Jake took only a moment longer to grab a shoulder holster with a Colt New Service revolver before running back to the kitchen.

The two women were huddled on the floor, and Annie still plied him with questions, but he didn't have time to answer as he shoved the .45 six-shooter into her hand.

"I'm sending Nub in. Crawl to the phone and get some help!"

Draping the bandolier over his shoulder, he stumbled over Lupe's outstretched legs and raced out onto the porch. He levered a cartridge into the carbine's chamber and saw a stationary rider down by the postmaster's house. The sunburst glinted from the gold buttons of a uniform as the Mexican raised his arm in signal.

"Kill all the *Americanos*!" the bandit shouted in Spanish, a language Jake knew well.

Throwing the carbine against his shoulder, Jake steadied himself against a porch post and fired. The rider was almost a hundred yards away, the limit of a Marlin's range, but down the sights Jake watched Gold Buttons tumble back out of the saddle, spooking his horse.

It was a hell of a thing, watching an enemy die by your own hand. Had it been a sister, it would have been all the more damnable. Yet on that long-ago day, even the latter would have been preferable.

Bullets began to whiz past, drawing Jake back to the here and now. He glimpsed Nub rushing out of his room with a pump-action shotgun, but Jake's attention was on the reports coming from nine o'clock and straight ahead. He may have dispatched one raider, but thirty-nine more sons of perdition were still out there.

"Foreman! Get in the house!" Jake said. "Cover the back windows!"

He didn't have time to see if Nub made it, for splinters flew from the post beside Jake's cheek and he retreated to his right down the porch. All the way, slugs peppered the adobe wall at his shoulder and raised puffs of dirt. Diving off the porch's far end, he twisted around on his hip so he could take a bead with his carbine around the corner post.

He didn't know what had happened to the yardman Alfonso, but from behind each shielding wall of adobe — the corral, the sheds, the well house — Jake could see muzzle flashes and curling smoke. The porch was underpinned by mud brick, protecting him to a degree, and the fact that he rested in a nook a few feet short of the corner of the house should have safeguarded his back. But with each bullet that struck the wall behind him, adobe shards buzzed past his ear.

Jake didn't have a clear target, but he fired a deterrence shot, and then another. He and Annie and the others were hopelessly out-numbered, just as he and his family had been in Mason County, and it was vital that they hold the house. He took heart when he heard a shotgun go off inside, for it told him that Nub was covering the rear.

From around the corner came a sudden drum of hoofs, and Jake turned and found the breast of a horse almost upon him. The rider would have gunned him down, but from the side of the house a revolver roared and the horse pulled away. As the hoofbeats receded, Jake was thankful that Annie kept watch on the kitchen window with that .45.

For what seemed forever, Jake held his position, firing and taking fire. With a Marlin, he could squeeze off a shot every five seconds, but his rounds weren't unlim-ited, forcing him to measure out his re-sponse. In truth, only a couple of minutes may have passed before volleys began to rain down hell on him from two o'clock. He was totally without protection, except the persuasion of return gunfire, and the bullets exploded with dreadful frequency against the mud bricks behind him. The debris pelted his shoulder, his hip, his ribs, and just as he threw another .44 Special round into the chamber, something branded his nose.

Jake cried out in pain and instinctively buried his head in the underpinning. An instant later a ricochet screamed by, and he scrambled to the porch and ran for the kitchen.

"I'm comin' in!" he warned.

He hoped he didn't meet a muzzle, but he didn't have time to worry about it. Good God, the bullets were thudding against the wall, even as they somehow missed him.

He fell inside the open door and rolled out of the line of fire. He came up on his hip with the carbine and peered around the jamb. The adobe walls were a foot thick, strong enough to withstand anything the Mexicans might have. But Jake and Nub could lay down only so much withering fire, and if the bandits chose to face it, they could overrun the house in moments.

Jake looked back over his shoulder. Lupe was sprawled under the table, a butcher knife in her hand. Beside the broken window on the left, Annie crouched at the ready with the .45 New Service revolver cocked, and Jake blurted a critical question.

"You call anybody?"

"Line ees dead, *señor!*" said Lupe.

Annie looked back. "They must have cut the — Jake! Your face is bleeding!"

Maybe so, but Jake had bigger concerns. In the next instant, a shotgun boomed from a back room, followed by Nub's frantic summons.

"Need help!"

Jake couldn't leave the front unguarded, and he alerted Annie before belly-crawling through the line of fire to the nearer bedroom. Framed in the doorway of Jake's bedroom of the night before, Nub was down on a knee, brandishing his shotgun from the hip as he tried to protect both rooms. Drawn to some unseen threat, the young man spun away and discharged his weapon.

The blast still rang in Jake's ears when he heard the tinkle of breaking glass on his left, and he whirled and fired through the iron latticework of a bed's headboard set flush against the jagged side window. He didn't think he hit anything, but he caught sight of a brute form as it withdrew.

From Jake's position just outside the kitchen, he could look back between the cookstove and table and out the front door. Eighty yards past the splintered porch post, a bandit was down off his horse, and Jake fired a quick shot that kicked up dust at his feet and chased him back to cover. Jake would have fired again, but his carbine's hammer clicked on empty and he had to set about reloading from the bandolier.

"An Eighth Cavalry officer was here before Thanksgiving," spoke up Nub. "He reaffirmed the safety of the immediate area."

"I got told the same thing."

A bullet pinged against the cast-iron stove, an unnecessary reminder that the Army had been wrong.

"They . . . They must disperse," Nub added. "Before the train reaches Valentine, the raiders must withdraw."

Jake knew what he meant. The girls would be riding the road from Valentine, and they would be alone in a country overrun with hostiles.

"Got to show 'em they can't whip us," he said. "How you fixed on shells?"

"Stuffed my pockets, Mr. Graves."

In all the times Jake had been around the Cross C foreman, he had never heard Nub call him "Mr. Graves" before, or any name whatsoever. Was this damned Indian already practicing for the family dynamics when he married Dru?

Jake slid a .44 Special cartridge down the

carbine's magazine. "Hope it's buckshot you got."

"Birdshot, I fear."

"Birdshot? Way things are on the border?"

"I've been hunting quail, sir."

Quail, my eye, thought Jake. And what was this "sir" stuff?

Jake ducked as a bullet ricocheted through the room. "Quail don't shoot back."

"Indeed, they do not," agreed Nub.

Nub's diction and command of the English language had never bothered Jake before, but now it aggravated the hell out of him. So *what* if this uppity Indian had gone away to Carlisle Indian School . . . Did he think he could show up a white man with a few slick words? And this coming from someone named Nub?

Jake felt his face flush hot. "What kind of name is 'Nub' for a growed man, anyway?" he challenged.

"My father —"

"The Apache one?"

"No, the only one I knew. Sam DeJarnett. I believe the two of you are acquainted." The foreman turned away briefly to scan the back bedroom with the shotgun. "He called me Nubbin when I was small. As I grew older it was abridged to Nub."

With nine new cartridges in place, Jake

levered one into the chamber and peered out the front door. "Your mama's a squaw, ain't she?"

Jake knew he might be provoking trouble that they didn't need when lives were on the line. But the foreman took it in stride.

"She's from three worlds," he said. "Mexican, Mescalero, and white."

"She don't know *what* she is, then," goaded Jake, watching for movement past the porch.

"My uncle Arch Brannon said she represents the best of each culture."

Jake glanced at him. "That Ranger in A Company way back? The one that talked like a schoolteacher?"

"He's not actually my uncle, but I grew up calling him that on the Singing Waters spread. He tutored me between his ranch duties until he arranged for my matriculation at Carlisle."

Jake wanted to ask what *matriculation* meant, but he didn't want to give an Indian a reason to feel superior. Especially after what Annie had told him.

A rider darted left to right across the sights of Jake's carbine, and Jake swung the barrel with the course of his flight and fired. He missed, but he raised a plume of dust from the bedroll behind the cantle of the saddle.

"A mama like yours," said Jake, still watching down the barrel, "makes you a regular duke's mixture, don't it? Indian, Mex'can, and God knows what else. What is it you call yourself?"

"A man, Mr. Graves. Just a man."

Jake turned, and two allies who hadn't come to terms about Dru stared at one another through the swirling gun smoke of a ranch under siege.

CHAPTER 2

The day wore on as sporadic gunfire kept Jake and the others pinned in the main residence. Repeatedly he would see bandits run to the storefront and spend a few seconds vainly trying to gain entry before retreating. Although the establishment was out of range for Jake's carbine, the raiders seemed unwilling to risk their lives for long against the possibility of a high-arcing scratch shot.

Finally, in the afternoon, a voice with a thick Spanish accent called from across the grounds.

"*Señores! Señores!* It is Alfonso!"

Jake glanced back at Nub, who was down on a knee in the threshold of the far bedroom. Taking advantage of a lull in the fighting, the foreman was reloading his pump-action Stevens — a six-shot model, Jake believed — with 12-gauge shells.

"That sound like your yardman?" Jake asked.

"Indeed. He can hear better from your position, Mr. Graves. Inquire if they have injured him."

Alfonso called again, and Jake studied the grounds through the open front door and tried to locate the young hand. He saw nothing out of the ordinary except the body of the dead man — the gold buttons of the uniform shining brighter than ever — but that didn't mean there weren't plenty of rifles trained in Jake's direction.

"*¿Estas bien,* Alfonso?" Jake shouted. "They hurt you any?"

"*Por favor,* don't shoot the bullets! I come to *la casa!* Don't shoot the bullets!"

Stepping out from behind his mud-plastered *jacal,* the boy of sixteen began to approach, his stride hesitant, halting. Even from a distance, Jake could see fear in his face. With every step, the *muchacho* glanced back, obviously expecting the same thing of the bandits as Jake did.

"They'll shoot him in the back!" Jake growled.

But there wasn't a damned thing he could do about it, except watch down the barrel and hope that a gunman's head popped out long enough to put a .44 Special slug through it.

"Jake?" Annie called from the kitchen. "What's happening, Jake?"

"We'll know in a minute. You and Lupe stay where you are, watch the window."

Jake had heard the in-laws say that the Cross C's was the only home Alfonso had known since losing his entire family down on the Rio Grande. The *muchacho* should have been working right now. He should have been going about his chores for fifty cents a day without having to worry about Carranza or Villa or anything else. But there he was, a terrified *muchacho* of Mexican heritage with both trouser knees torn, continuing his slow advance and providing cruel amusement for a den of snakes.

But to Jake's surprise, Alfonso made it to the base of the porch steps. With another look back, the *muchacho* stopped, his ashen cheek twitching and his lips trembling. There was blood in his ear, and he kept his right arm against his ribs as he winced with every breath.

"Get inside!" said Jake.

"¡*Venga pronto,* Alfonso!" Nub added. "You are permitted!"

But the *muchacho* only stood shaking, unable or unwilling to come closer. Down the rifle barrel, Jake scanned the grounds over the boy's shoulder.

"Make it damned quick!" he urged.

"They kill me I go on porch." The *mucha-cho's* knees were quaking, but so was his voice. "Bad *hombre* tell me so."

"He in charge?" asked Jake.

"They call him *capitán. Muy* tall." Alfonso touched both sides of his face and neck. "Leper spots *aquí.* He send me to talk."

"Rentería!" said Jake.

The *muchacho's* face went white. "Santa Maria!" he whispered with a look back. "Now I know him!"

A onetime Carrancista officer, Jesús Rentería had been discharged for cruelties too heinous for even Carranza's Constitutionalist Army. Jake had heard one troubling story of a captive woman placed in the middle of a corral with Carrancistas sitting on the surrounding fence. At Rentería's signal, the troops had raced for the captive, and the first man to seize her had won the right to violate her as the others watched.

"A *brujo* from a land of *brujos!*" added Alfonso. "*Mi papá* say this about Rentería!"

"Witch, hell," said Jake. "A bastard's all he is."

"He have *magia negra,* too strong for even *curandera!*"

Witches, black magic, folk healers — Jake

32

had more pressing worries right now.

"What's he want?"

"He say tell you surr . . . How you say, surr . . ."

"Surrender? You tell him to go to hell."

"You say no, they bomb *la casa,*" said the *muchacho.* "He tell me so."

"Let 'em fly at it!" Jake reiterated. "This is a fight to the finish!"

When his declaration was met with stony silence by Nub, Jake looked back at him. "You with me on this?"

The foreman wrinkled his brow. "They have a considerable force. This bomb they speak of . . ."

"Hell, if you don't want to fight, I'll do it by myself."

With a wag of his head, Jake turned back to the kitchen door. He couldn't look in on Annie without exposing himself to gunfire, but his voice could go places with no heed for consequences.

Or maybe not, considering what he heard himself say.

"Your golden-haired boy's ready to give up, Annie. Never figured him for a —"

"Sir, you're mischaracterizing my stance," interrupted Nub. "I merely sought more information."

Jake glanced back. "You'd still be thinkin'

on it and they'd have the whole house over-run. If they got a bomb, they'd use it instead of talkin'. You ever give —"

"Stop it, Jake!" he heard Annie say. "Drucilla's on her way with Ruthie!"

Jake didn't want to think about it. Lord Almighty, his daughter and niece, headed straight for a firefight. Even worse, the moment Rentería saw the two he would start slobbering in anticipation like the damned cur he was.

Jake gripped the Marlin so tightly that it shook.

"We got to fight them off before they get here," he said hoarsely, peering past Alfonso. "If we don't ever do another thing, we got to fight them off in time."

He didn't expect Nub to speak up, but the foreman did so.

"I trust your judgment, Mr. Graves. What-ever happens, we cannot subject Dru and Miss Ruthie to this."

Even in his expression of support, the damned Indian had found a way to show disrespect. *Dru and Miss Ruthie.* What gave him the right to speak of Dru in so familiar a way, while reserving a polite title for Ruthie?

Addressing Alfonso again, Jake repeated his go-to-hell message for Rentería, and the shaken *muchacho* turned away with glistening cheeks and started back across the compound, the cuffs of his baggy pants dragging at his heels. Jake felt for the boy, knowing that an animal like Rentería might kill the messenger because he didn't like the answer. As Jake's frustration and anger grew, he turned and took it out on the only person he could.

"You watchin' that back window?" he asked Nub. "How you see anything, way you squint your eyes?"

The foreman did have an unusual pinch to his eyes, no matter if it was day or night.

"Look half asleep all time," Jake added. "Won't they open no wider?"

"They've served me well to this point, sir."

Jake wanted to ask, *Then why can't you see that Dru's white and you ain't?* But Annie was listening and Nub didn't give him a chance.

"I'm informed that my first name was Little Squint Eyes," the foreman quickly added.

"Little *what*?"

"It's a translation of a Mescalero name you might find onerous."

Jake gave a caustic half-laugh. "Nobody done you any favors in the namin', did they."

For Annie's sake, Jake knew he should let

the matter go, but he couldn't stop himself. "Nub, Nubbin, Little Squint Eyes," Jake mused out loud. "Don't know which is worse."

Annie had heard enough.

"All you do is criticize him! Just so he can shoot, Jake! Now quit it!" Then she addressed the one who stood to be their son-in-law. "Nub, he's all wrought up and taking it out on you. He doesn't mean anything by it."

The hell I don't, thought Jake.

" 'Men in rage strike those that wish them best,' " said Nub.

Jake went quiet for a moment, wondering if it was an insult. "Do what?"

"Iago in *Othello,*" said the foreman. "Shakespeare."

Down on the river where Jake had worked, even pulp magazines didn't circulate, much less Shakespeare. But he had other concerns now, for Alfonso had stopped at the *jacal's* far end, where rough hands reached out and dragged him out of sight behind a mud wall burnished by the sunlight.

Any second, a gunshot would echo across the yard, and Alfonso would sink to the ground. Or maybe the *muchacho's* end would come in terrible silence, except for his gurgles as Rentería drew a knife across his throat. Either way the boy would be just as dead, another victim in a border war that didn't care how many innocents it claimed. And when the assault on the main residence resumed, it would be only a matter of time before Jake and Nub were also dead — leaving Annie and Lupe defenseless in face of something unimaginable.

The anticipation was a form of torture, growing worse as the stillness persisted for a full minute, and then two and three. Eventually, a shout broke the menacing hush — a shout that Jake recognized as Alfonso's voice. The *muchacho* gave warning that he was stepping into the open, and a moment later he was there, appearing no worse than before as he began to approach.

Again, he made it just shy of the porch steps before stopping.

"*El brujo* say, you don't shoot the bullets, they don't shoot the bullets," related the *muchacho.* "He want keys to store."

Jake looked back at Nub.

"Lupe?" asked the foreman in response. "Might a set of keys be here?"

"*¿Quién sabe?*" the cook replied from the kitchen. "Who knows?"

Jake turned back to the *muchacho.* "There's a ax by the woodpile. They can break in with it. Hurry up!"

"*El brujo* say he want *los caballos* too."

"Show 'em the saddle horses. ¡*Vaya con prisa!*"

With each of the boy's measured strides, the jog trot of Dru's horse would be eating up the distance, drawing her closer to the Cross C's in the company of her cousin. Couldn't the *muchacho* walk any faster? He almost seemed in slow motion as he veered to the woodpile, and once there, the seconds passed like hours as he tried to extricate the buried ax head from a log. Finally, ax in hand, he continued on across the yard and disappeared around the *jacal.*

"They'll leave now, won't they, Jake?" asked Annie. "They'll take what they want and leave, won't they?"

He didn't know what to tell her. All Rentería had to gain by raiding the Cross C's were horses and provisions, but he was a devil — maybe not a *brujo,* a witch, as Alfonso had said — but a devil nonetheless, and someone who had perpetrated such evil in that corral couldn't be outthought.

"Jake," pressed Annie, "what's going to come of things? What's going to come of . . . Drucilla and Ruthie? They'll be all right, won't they?"

Jake had never lied to Annie, and he wouldn't do so now, even if he had to ignore her. Anyway, there was something else on his mind, and he turned to Nub. For a moment, as the foreman looked back at him with the dark eyes of an Apache, Jake would have gladly accepted the idea of Dru in Nub's arms if it meant she were safe.

"The old storekeep's name," Jake said. "Gadsden?"

"He resides just beyond the store."

"I suppose he's got keys, don't he? Did you hear what that man I shot was hollerin'? Kill the *Americanos*? I was afraid to sic that bunch on a white man. Hope the ax does the trick."

"Indeed. Mr. Gadsden is such a soft-spoken man and so mild in manner."

Jake breathed sharply. "Just the kind bullies like pushin' around."

"In the winter past, his wife persuaded him to relocate to San Antonio to be with their son. Before they could accomplish it, she was stricken by pneumonia. Upon her death, he asked that she be interred outside his window so she would be close during the night. After fifty years together, he intends to remain here until he can join her."

Jake could just imagine trying to go on without Annie. "Life don't always go like you planned it, does it," he said quietly.

"At least they were permitted a life together."

Once more, Jake briefly studied this unwelcome suitor of Dru's, and the unspoken between them was more powerful than anything they might have said.

Still, there were more urgent matters. A cease-fire was meaningless to men without honor, but Jake wanted to widen his view of the grounds, even at the risk of catching a bullet. Rolling into the kitchen, he regained his earlier position beside the open door. From where he stood with his shoulder against adobe, he watched riders and men afoot gather at the store. They were a motley bunch: swarthy men in wide-brimmed sombreros or no hats at all, ragged coats or slouchy woolen sweaters, unkempt Carrancista uniforms or the soiled cotton garments of peons. All they had in common were crisscrossed bandoliers and the glint of sunlight in carbines and in the *pistolas* and knives at their waists.

The way Jake remembered the store, the wooden door was thick and steel-banded. As with the bars across the windows, it had been designed to deter unauthorized entry, but right now Jake wished the door were as fragile as an apple crate. Soon, a short, stocky bandit set to work on it with the ax, and the *pop! pop! pop!* was like a clock tolling off the seconds that brought Dru and Ruthie closer and closer.

The door resisted, and the frustrated Mexican stepped aside and let another bandit take over. But his efforts proved just as futile, and when a third man took up the task, he pointed out something about the ax handle. A crack must have developed, for the first time he swung it, the head broke off.

Tempers flared, the swear words flying, and things grew worse when the door held firm against the man's repeated kicks. Someone shoved him aside and threw an ineffective shoulder into the wood, but one shove led to another until a dozen bandits swarmed like yellowjackets.

Into the fight waded a figure half a head taller than anyone else. Jake couldn't see his features, but he had to be Rentería, considering how his presence squelched the melee. After inspecting the door, the *capitán* gestured for Alfonso and dispatched the *muchacho* to the main residence a third time.

"*El brujo* say give him keys and open safe or he kill everybody," Alfonso said upon stopping before the porch steps.

Jake turned to Annie. She still stood beside the broken window, the sparkling edges of jagged glass throwing sunlight in her face. There was grave concern in her hazel eyes as she looked back at him, and Jake realized that she understood his dilemma. Did he send the bandits to Gadsden's home, knowing what they might do to the merchant? But to do otherwise might mean an all-out assault, and neither a carbine nor a shotgun nor the revolver at Annie's apron would be enough.

Then Annie said two words, "The girls!" and Jake knew what he had to do.

He spun to Alfonso. "Take the *bandidos* to the storekeep's house. Mr. Gadsden, savvy? Run this time! Run!"

Maybe a run was too much to ask of someone who had been roughed up, but the *muchacho* did his best. After disappearing beyond the *jacal,* he remained out of view until he reemerged in the distance at a point out of carbine range. A horde of bandits escorted him as he veered for Gadsden's home. From Jake's perspective, the store in the foreground hid most of the house, except for a whitewashed wall with a mound and cross below.

Jake couldn't help but wonder if a second grave would mark the spot sooner than anyone had expected.

"I hope to hell I done right," he muttered.

"You arrived at the only prudent course of action, Mr. Graves," Nub said from behind. "The greater good demanded it."

Maybe so. But Jake didn't need someone like Nub to tell him.

Soon the bandits reappeared, the sun shining on the old storekeeper's balding pate and dancing on his keys as a squat Mexican in sombrero prodded him along at rifle point. Jake could only imagine what had taken place out of sight, but Gadsden's bloody face and stumbling gait told him all he needed to know.

After the merchant unlocked the store, the tall raider who Jake presumed to be Rentería pushed him through the open door. The *capitán* was the first raider inside, but a dozen more rushed in at his heels.

"They're in," said Jake.

Digging into his pants pocket, Jake withdrew his gold-plated watch by its leather fob and checked the time. A gift from Annie on their thirtieth anniversary, the open-face Hamilton had cost her $12.25, two weeks' wages for a ranch hand. He had chided her for the extravagance, but she had countered that the twenty-year warranty on the case meant that the gold wouldn't wear through to the underlying brass until they celebrated their fiftieth anniversary.

As Jake studied the small dial inset over the 6, however, he wouldn't have cared if the sweeping second hand had already broken. Each tick was too much like the beat of a scythe swishing back and forth against the sky and dropping lower over Dru and Ruthie.

He looked up to find more raiders congregating at the store.

"They gotta leave," he wished out loud. "They gotta take what they want and get out of here."

"I-I'm so uneasy about things," said Annie. The deep emotion in her voice drew his gaze. "The girls, they —"

"We's done all we can."

"Will . . . Will you pray with me, darlin'?"

Jake shuddered to the memory of his sister down the sights of a Sharp's carbine.

"You's always been the one for that sort of thing, Annie. Learned when I was sixteen wasn't no use me doin' it. If anybody up there cares, I hope He listens better to you than He done for me."

Dru assumed that her mother had broken the news about Nub by now, but the prospect of facing a father with all his expectations and prejudices was still terrifying.

Over the dusty ears of her big dun, Dru

44

watched Capote Mountain rise and fall with the horse's jog trot across this high desert grassland with javelina bush and twisted Spanish daggers, spiny cholla and rattling sotol stalks. Capote's angling ridge, its sharp western face catching late afternoon sunlight, had dominated the south horizon for miles, but now it seemed close enough to reach out and touch.

And Dru still didn't know how to steel herself for the impending glare of her father's gray eyes.

With her cousin Ruthie — at twenty-one, two years her junior — Dru had stepped off a Southern Pacific train in Valentine after a 36-mile trip from Marfa. Valentine was the shipping point for the Cross C's, and the ranch always stabled a few horses in the small town as a convenience. Away to the south at Ruthie's home at Cross C headquarters, eighteen miles by a seldom-used road from Valentine, awaited a Christmas get-together that threatened to be as much a confrontation as a celebration. Soon the girls had struck out on horses rigged for cow work, and now they had put a lot of miles behind them.

Even absent the matter of Nub, Dru knew that her father would have reason to be displeased when she showed up with a high-topped cowboy boot in each stirrup. Wearing men's duck trousers would concern him enough, but for his daughter to straddle a horse was out of the question. Wanting her raised a lady like her mother, a mannerly schoolteacher, he had bought Dru a brown bengaline riding habit suitable for a side-saddle. She hadn't dare tell him that she had been riding astride on the Cross C's with Ruthie.

"The most docile Cross C horses," Nub had told the girls, "remain broncs subject to intemperate behavior. Deep saddles are a requisite to avert dislodgment."

Ruthie had giggled at Nub's professor-like explanation. "That means our broncs take a hankerin' to swallowin' their heads and dumpin' you on your rump, Dru."

To say "rump" in mixed company just wasn't done, and Dru had never been so embarrassed. But Ruthie delighted in such things, and she maintained her reputation as she rode abreast on Dru's right on this Christmas afternoon.

"So will y'all's children talk like you, or like Nub?" Ruthie asked, her curly blond hair bouncing with her bay's gait.

"You're insufferable, talking about children already. The very idea!"

Dimples creased Ruthie's cheeks as she

46

smiled mischievously. "Hmmm. *Insufferable.* You must've picked that up from Nub when y'all rode to Capote Falls by yourselves."

"Ruthie Cowan, don't you dare tell Dad. He'd have a conniption if he knew we were alone like that."

"If Aunt Annie's already told him about Nub, he'll have a good idea you two's been alone sometime or other. Has Nub kissed you yet?"

"Ruthie! I'll take this quirt to you!"

"Mama says she never kissed Daddy till they was married. So what's it like, kissin'?"

"None of your business! Go kiss somebody yourself if you want to find out."

"Daddy would shoot Nub, if it was him. He'd blow his top and say no Mex'can or Indian was goin' to take advantage of *his* daughter, and he'd shoot him."

Dru drew rein, inducing her cousin to do the same.

"That's not funny, Ruthie," she said, looking at the girl framed between two Spanish daggers just off the road. "That's not funny at all."

"Daddy says he's never knowed anybody as smart as Nub but he's still got to keep him in his place."

"He's trusted him with the bookkeeping all this time, and now he's his foreman."

"Oh, I like Nub and all, Dru. Don't get me wrong. But Nub can't never scrub the Mex'can off of him, or Indian either, like Daddy says. I expect Uncle Jake thinks the same way."

Dru looked down at the saddle horn and her voice dropped. "He can't go back and change who his parents were. What's Dad expect him to do?"

"That's just it, Dru. Way Daddy tells it, we's supposed to stay what we are. He says God made all nations of men and set the bounds of their habitation. Workin' with each other's okay, but it can't go no further."

"My hair's as dark as Nub's is," Dru contended.

"But your skin ain't."

Dru had heard more than she wanted. "It's not like Nub's colored," she asserted, more to herself than to Ruthie. "There's no law."

"Daddy's law — Uncle Jake's too, probably — is a whole lot stricter."

Dru liked the impish Ruthie better than the serious one. Urging the dun on down the road for the Cross C's, Dru now dreaded getting there more than ever. For a minute or two there was only the rhythm of eight hoofs in trot, and then a new worry seized her and she studied her cousin

48

against the passing sotol stalks.

"You didn't say anything to your folks, I don't guess."

" 'Bout you and Nub? Of course not. Best friends keep secrets. Well, guess it ain't a secret no more, if your dad's found out. The news will be all over the country by the time my parents get back."

Dru didn't like the sound of that. Why did the way she and Nub felt about each other have to cause such a fuss?

"They won't hold it against Nub, will they?" Dru asked. "He won't lose his job or anything?"

"Daddy's awful set in his ways. I imagine it'll all be up to how Uncle Jake takes things."

That wasn't very encouraging to Dru, and as she fixed her gaze on the approaching ridge of Capote, she wondered for the first time if she and Nub had made a mistake. But things had a way of just happening sometimes.

From the moment they had met three years ago — she on the headquarters porch, and Nub below the steps with his hat in his hands — she had felt a connection. She had been smitten by his intelligence and politeness, and his shy, boyish way even though he had been much older. After that encounter, she had looked forward to visiting Ruthie on the Cross C's more than ever, despite the teasing by Ruthie whenever Nub had found another trifling reason to come to headquarters during one of Dru's stays.

Then a few months ago, the three of them had planned a ride along the base of Capote ridge and on to Capote Falls. Ruthie, perhaps playing matchmaker to stir up things for her amusement, had complained of illness at the last moment and had urged them to go on without her. A rattler, a runaway horse, and a strong arm that had plucked Dru from the saddle in the nick of time — things had just happened, all right, and as soon as Nub had lowered her to the ground and dismounted beside her, nature had taken its course.

Yes, Ruthie needed to learn for herself what it was like to be kissed.

After that moment, the relationship had advanced rapidly until, as Nub stated, "it seems inconceivable that we should be apart."

And yet there might be forces bent on that very injustice.

Dru and Nub had talked about it some, especially the resistance she expected from her father. But only now did she realize that not only might Nub lose his job, but the respect of any other white rancher in these parts. What kind of future was that for a caring person who happened to be Apache and Mexican?

"You think Uncle Jake's already lit into Nub?"

Ruthie wasn't one to let a delicate matter go, even as Dru had gone silent on this Christmas Day.

"Why do you have to say things like that?" reproached Dru.

"Talkin' about it ain't goin' to keep it from happenin'. Daddy says Uncle Jake's tough as old saddle leather."

"Not when Mama's around."

"She can't be around all time. Think Nub will hold his ground?"

Dru hoped so, because it might earn him respect. After all, her father had served the cause of justice up and down the river for a lot of years, and he couldn't have done so without being a good judge of character. She just hoped that he wouldn't be blinded by intolerance when it involved his daughter.

"You sure you thought on this real hard?" pressed Ruthie. "You don't think there ain't somebody else out there for you instead?"

Dru looked at her.

"We just passed the turnoff to the Capps

place," Ruthie went on. She glanced back — almost wistfully, thought Dru. "The young one's awful good-lookin'. Not married neither."

"Dad said don't ever go by there, no matter what. He had some trouble with Mr. Capps down on the river."

"Bo's different though," Ruthie contended. "Not ever' son takes after his pa. He's —"

"Stop it, Ruthie."

"Oh, well, if you don't want Bo, I'll take him for myself. Livin' so close, he's sweet on me, you know."

"Sweet on you? How long's *this* been going on? How come you haven't told me?"

Ruthie placed a finger across her lips. "Shhh! You ain't the only one with a big secret, Drucilla Graves!" She smiled merrily.

Dru could never tell when Ruthie was serious, but she played along with her.

"And here you are, asking me what it's like to kiss!" Dru said.

Ruthie giggled. "Bo don't have a brother, but maybe he's got a cousin. Think of it, Dru. We could *both* marry into the family."

Dru's gaiety faded. "You know how I feel about Nub," she said seriously.

"Oh, Nub's good-lookin' — for what he

is, anyway — and he's nice and all, but you might do like my mother says. Tally up the pluses and minuses and see where things stand."

In the distance, just out of the shadow of imposing Capote ridge, Dru distinguished for the first time the sun-splashed specks of white that had to be the buildings at Cross C headquarters. It was almost too late for ciphering, but for night after sleepless night, Dru had lain in bed and done exactly as Ruthie had suggested.

There were more minuses to marrying Nub than she could count, and they affected everyone in her life or who might someday be a part of it. Most importantly, they impacted her mother and father and could have lifelong consequences for any children with whom God might bless the union. And as Ruthie had just made her realize, Nub might even lose his position and struggle to find another job worthy of his abilities.

The minuses were overwhelming, a crushing set of cold, hard facts to guide Dru's actions. Meanwhile, she could think of only a single entry for the plus side of the ledger.

"You done figurin' yet?" asked Ruthie, drawing Dru's attention.

"It didn't help."

"How come? How many minuses and pluses you come up with?"

"It doesn't work that way, Ruthie. Some things are more important than others."

Ruthie twitched her nose as she often did when making mischief.

"Oh, I get it. You're wonderin' how many minuses a kiss can cancel out."

Well, Ruthie was close, anyway. A kiss in itself might not be worth much, but there was no way to place a value on the love behind it.

CHAPTER 3

Tick, tick, tick.

Any second now, Dru and Ruthie would ride into Cross C headquarters, and no matter how hard Jake stared at his pocket watch, he couldn't make time slow down.

Tick, tick, tick.

He felt equally helpless as he reconnoitered the store from just inside the main residence. The bandits, oblivious to time, persisted in their slow, methodical pillage. They came and went through the store's doorway in a steady stream as they traded shabby garments and worn footwear for new clothes and shiny Hamilton Brown shoes. Next, they began hauling out bulky linen sacks, obviously booty loaded into what had been fifty- and one-hundred-pound sacks of flour or other food items. Elsewhere, Jake could see raiders bring up the Cross C saddle stock, and he continued to watch as the Mexicans switched their saddles to the fresh animals and loaded the jaded horses with the sacked plunder.

Tick, tick, tick.

Dru and Ruthie, any second now . . .

Tick, tick, tick.

The raiders still taking their time . . .

At long last, the band assembled near the store: more than thirty able-bodied men already mounted, four gunshot victims hunched over saddle horns, and the dead man strapped facedown across a mule like a freshly killed hog.

Tick, tick, tick.

Ride, Jake begged silently, *you got to ride*!

He must have said it out loud without realizing, for Annie spoke from across the room.

"They're leaving, darlin'? Please tell me they're going!"

Even the tall man Jake believed to be Rentería was in the saddle now, one of the few men without a tow rope for a pack animal. Muffled hoofbeats suddenly called Jake's attention to the left of the porch and whatever was hidden behind Nub's wing of the residence, and a moment later a horse appeared where the Valentine road bent around the adobe corner.

Until Jake saw the bandit in the stirrups, he hadn't realized that the Mexicans had posted a sentry on the road. Now, all Jake could do was listen as the lookout shouted a terrifying alert.

Riders were upon them — two señoritas!

"God A'mighty!" Jake cried.

The lookout stayed visible only long enough for Rentería to signal to his troops. Then dust flew across the grounds as the sentry wheeled his animal back up the concealed road and a dozen of Rentería's riders broke from the assembled force and bolted after him.

Jake drowned out Annie's frantic words as he yelled to Nub. "The girls! Stop 'em at the back window!"

Jake could only wait and hope as he heard the foreman rush through the back bedroom, but it was already too late.

"Two Mexicans have intercepted them!" said Nub.

No!

All Jake could do for the moment was hold his position, for the residence was now in carbine range for the dozen approaching riders as they veered for the Valentine road around the wing of the residence.

"Help them girls!" he shouted to Nub. "If you got a shot, take it!"

"The bandits are seeking the bridles! Twelve-gauge shot would strike everyone!"

"What's —"

"Dru repelled them with her quirt!" Nub interrupted. "The girls are taking flight around the wing of the house!"

Decency and evil were about to collide on the grounds of the Cross C's, and Jake felt a pair of events forty-seven years apart begin to merge.

From around the corner, Dru and her dun burst into sight, a stride ahead of Ruthie and her bay. But Rentería's riders were there to meet them, and as everyone drew rein, the dust caught up and fell over the scene like a shroud. Jake may have called Dru's name, but all he knew for sure as the dust cleared was that bandits had seized the bridles of both girls' horses.

"Let 'em go!" he yelled. "You got what you want! Let 'em go!"

The only reply was a revolver shot that exploded against the doorjamb. Jake ducked inside, the ricochet still singing, and when he came up with his .44 Special Marlin again, his instinct was to return fire. But there was no way to rescue the girls in a skirmish with fourteen bandits, even if almost twice that many hadn't stood at the ready two hundred yards away. All he could do was prevail on their sense of decency — but what decency could men like these have?

58

"Rentería!" Jake called across the grounds. Even among mounted troops as far away as the store, the tall *capitán* was conspicuous. "We ain't fired a shot more! We done what you said! Let the girls be!"

Was that laughter Jake could hear from all that distance? It seemed to come from only Rentería at first, but three dozen men, far and near, quickly took it up — an unmistakable sign that Jake's greatest fears were about to be realized.

Ruthie was crying hysterically, but Dru wouldn't give up without a fight. Turning her quirt on the bandit who held her horse, she flogged him in the face with the leather braids before another rider clutched her arm and confiscated the whip.

Annie couldn't see any of this, and a resumption of withering gunfire made Jake's ears ring, but she obviously could hear the girls' cries of distress.

"Do something, Jake!" Annie pleaded. "Don't let them carry them off! Jake! Jake!"

Pinned down, Jake could only manage glimpses of the bandits when they withdrew with the girls toward the store. But as they bore across the grounds, shooting back as they rode, the change in angle allowed him enough protection to look down the sights of his Marlin around the doorjamb.

He didn't like what he saw.

Rider after rider crowded two innocent girls as they rushed them away toward an unthinkable end. A small army it was, straight out of hell, and there was nothing in the world Jake could do to stop this.

Except . . .

He abruptly found the sights swaying against a girlish form, and then another. His daughter and niece were there, Dru's black hair and Ruthie's blond tresses playing between their respective shoulder blades.

As heavy as his father's Sharps had been forty-seven years earlier, the six-pound carbine now seemed heavier. Strange, the impressions that came to him: the solid-wood stock in his cheek, the butt plate in his shoulder, the grip sweaty in his hand. Never before had Jake been so conscious of his three fingers inside the lever's oblong port. Already they were twitching, ready to eject the first spent shell and throw another cartridge into the chamber. But nothing dominated like the cocked hammer at his face and his finger sweaty against a trigger ready to kill.

And to save.

But could he find the courage to do what he hadn't as a sixteen-year-old?

"Shoot her! You got to shoot her!"

60

They were his mother's words, following him across all the years since Mason County, but they must have been Jake's words as well on this Christmas Day in 1917.

"You cannot!"

A sudden force drove the rifle barrel upward, the muzzle clipping the door head above. The jolt forced Jake to squeeze the trigger, the carbine roaring at point-blank range against wood. Chips and adobe debris rained down, but he was already twisting around to a hovering figure in a leather vest.

"You cannot!" Nub said again.

Jake elbowed him in the chest. "Get the hell away!"

He spun again to the door and took a bead across the grounds, but Dru and Ruthie were already out of range. He watched in frustration and terrible rage as the two troops merged, swallowing not only his niece, but the daughter who meant more to him and Annie than anything in the world.

Jake whirled on Nub. "You had no right! No right!"

"You would have killed her! You would have dispatched them both!"

"My right to decide! Not yours!"

"They took her, Jake?" spoke up Annie.

"Oh Lord, they carried them off?"

Nub was trembling as he turned to Annie. "Had I not intervened she would be dead, Mrs. Graves. My Dru and Miss —"

Jake shoved him in the chest. "Your Dru, hell! You disrespectful . . . !"

Nub stumbled back and fell across the table, knocking pans to the floor.

"Stop it!" pleaded Annie, so distraught that Jake could barely understand her. "Please stop it!"

Jake stepped back and looked toward the store again. Through the big yucca beyond, the riders were striking out toward the sinking sun in the west-southwest, where three miles away the Rim's serrated range was a blight across the bottom of the sky.

"Is . . . Is Nub right, Jake?" he heard Annie ask. "Were you fixing to kill our . . . our . . ."

Jake turned, knowing he would have to face her sooner or later.

"I-I don't know," he said with cracked voice. "Maybe. I-I don't know."

"Darlin'," she appealed. *"Oh, darlin'!"*

Jake's eyes began to sting, but he could still read the disbelief in her face as she placed fingers at her temples and broke down.

"Our little girl, our little girl!" she sobbed.

"What are we going to do?"

Jake rushed across the room and pulled her close, and for a moment he wept with her. Then he withdrew and looked into her stunned eyes.

"Them devils is headed for the border, Annie. You and Lupe get over to the neighbors and call for help. You're safe, so let me have the six-shooter. I'll chase 'em on foot if I have to!"

Taking the holstered .45, Jake ran to the door without so much as a glance at Nub, but the foreman's voice caught up with him on the porch.

"I join you as a soldier in the same cause, Mr. Graves!"

"I cannot believe what he would have done."

Time was critical, but Nub paused with his hand on the doorjamb and spoke as he looked back at Dru's mother. He had never seen anyone so distressed, and it showed in her blanched cheeks and trembling lips, her welling eyes and quaking chin. Even more troubling, he could see Dru in her features — the Dru whose fear must have grown into sheer terror by now.

"I cannot believe a father could perpetrate an act so heinous," Nub added.

It took a moment for Annie to get her

voice to work. "You-you can't imagine how . . . how much he loves her, Nub. More than anything — *anything!*"

"Then how could he have —"

"There's things happened to him growing up you don't know."

"I fear for Dru's welfare and Miss Ruthie's. But now I must protect them from him as well as from the bandits."

He bolted out the door and off the porch, and he didn't look back even as she called after him.

As he rushed after Jake in the direction of the store, Nub already grieved for what he might not ever have — the thousands of tomorrows and the home and the love that only Dru could offer. He couldn't be denied it! He *couldn't,* even if he had to do as Jake had suggested and overtake the bandits by foot. Indeed, Nub had the parentage for it, for in his veins flowed the blood of Apaches who had prided themselves in running great distances without rest.

Still, what could a lone man do in the face of an army, except what Jake had devised moments ago?

Nub was so shaken by the girls' abduction that he had almost forgotten about the lonely, grandfatherly man who was the storekeeper. But as he caught up with Jake outside Capote Store, in a spot piled high with merchandise the bandits had been unable to pack off, a troubling realization struck him.

Of the dozens of men who had entered the establishment, Gadsden alone had never come out.

"Mr. Gadsden!"

The summons was still on his lips when Nub burst through the doorway a step behind Dru's father, a whistling wind following. Footing was poor in the narrow salesroom, the floor rolling under Nub's boots, and as he came up at Jake's shoulder he understood why. Wanting linen sacks for the spoils, the raiders had emptied out hundreds of pounds of corn and dried beans.

Nub might as well not have existed for all the eye contact the older man made in a quick scan left and right. Nub looked too, finding the pillage destructive. Commodities cluttered the wraparound counters and overflowed to the floor, and the background shelves were all but stripped. The cash register was open, and so was the safe. Clothing, new and discarded, dangled from shelves and littered the floor. Down among the kernels of corn at Jake's heels were cartridges and shotgun shells.

"Gadsden! You in here?" called the older man.

When there was no answer, Jake rushed to the cash register and leaned over the counter to search underneath. At the counter across the salesroom, Nub did the same, knocking off crockery but finding nothing on the floor but scattered cans and new Hamilton Brown footwear.

"Gadsden!" Jake shouted again.

Nub had frequented Capote Store ever since signing on with the Cross C's, so he knew that the wareroom entrance was at the right end of the salesroom. Wading through the beans and corn, he opened a gate in the counter and edged past the seven-foot shelves. Beyond were more freestanding storage units, all of them plundered like the salesroom.

Abruptly, between tobacco tins at eye level on a shelf, Nub caught sight of movement ahead. A step in front of Dru's father, he broke around the final shelving and saw it silhouetted against a bright window.

A man's body. Hanging upside down by the ankles. Swinging ever so slightly, the taut rope creaking from a rafter.

But there was more, grisly and loathsome. From ear to ear, Gadsden's throat had been cut, and his twisting body hovered over a red pool that crept toward Nub's boots.

"My Lord," he gasped. "My Lord Almighty."

"The sons of hell!" exclaimed Jake. "Wasn't enough to kill him, they had to do it *this* way!"

Nub went weak in the knees. No gentler man had he ever known, and it grieved him to consider the storekeeper's final moments. His killer had even been so callous as to clean the bloody knife on the merchant's drooping white shirt.

"If . . . If they would perpetrate this against a man so mild, what might they do to . . . to . . ."

Nub couldn't manage the words.

A rough hand suddenly spun him around, and Nub looked into the gray eyes of a father in a rage.

"I could've stopped it!" said Jake. "What happens to them girls is *your* fault, ever' bit of it, here on out!"

Jake wheeled with a hard shove to Nub's shoulder and stalked away. Forced to take a step back, Nub righted himself, but as he followed, his boot was sticky with the blood of a lost man who would finally find peace beside a lonely grave.

As sickened as Nub was by the inhumanity, he was troubled even more by what Jake had said. Could Dru's father be right? Had Nub preserved the two girls' lives just so they could face a hell that would go on and on?

Dru! Dru! I sought only to help! Dru!

But Dru couldn't answer, and all Nub could do for now was glance back through empty shelves at the storekeeper's throat continuing to drip.

At the salesroom gate, Nub found Dru's father lifting a tin cup from the counter. There was something unusual about the mug, and Nub stepped closer and saw blood in the bottom. But Jake seemed more interested in another detail, and as he twisted the cup in inspection, Nub was struck by a red smear under the rim — the kind a woman might paint with her lipstick as she drank.

But neither cosmetics nor a woman had played any role in this.

"Good God," muttered Jake.

They whirled together toward Gadsden's concealed body.

"Are . . . Are we to construe . . ."

Nub had more to say, more questions to pose, but when he turned back, he saw Jake set the cup aside and drag a fifty-pound sack of flour across the counter.

"Let's get what we come for and get out

of here," the older man said, opening it with his pocketknife.

Sifted flour flew everywhere as he emptied the linen sack and stuffed it in Nub's hands.

"Canned goods, especially tomatoes," instructed Jake. "All you can carry."

More juice than substance, tomatoes were a staple in this desert that could dehydrate a man quickly in winter, and even as Nub considered the ramifications of the cup, he rushed about behind the counter, gathering what canned items he could find.

Looking up, he saw Jake rummaging in the salesroom floor for ammunition, and soon the former customs inspector's pockets and bandolier swelled. On a shelf under the counter, Nub discovered field glasses and slipped the strap around his neck. There were also three unopened containers of 12-gauge buckshot, and as soon as he added them to the linen sack, he joined Jake on the salesroom floor and accepted several shells of number 8 birdshot.

In the welcome sunshine outside the door, they met the young yardman, creeping along half bent over. The blood in his ear had dried, but he continued to hold his right arm against his ribs and wince with every breath.

"Alfonso!" said Nub. "Are you sound?

¿*Estas bien?*"

"*Sí, señor,*" the *muchacho* said unconvincingly.

"We's goin' after 'em!" spoke up Jake. "What about horses?"

"Do any remain?" elaborated Nub. "Might the far trap still have —"

"*Sí,* I show *bandidos* only close trap."

"We got to have mounts, bedrolls too," said Jake. "You bring us some if we start out afoot?"

"You're aware," added Nub, "that they have taken Miss Ruthie and her cousin?"

"*Lo siento,*" the *muchacho* said sorrowfully. "*El brujo muy* bad *hombre.* He kill *mi hermana,* my baby sister. She die *chupado por el brujo.*"

"Sucked by the witch?" translated Jake. "What's that mean?"

"Rentería feed on babies. *Señoritas* too."

"What the hell you talkin' about?"

While Jake was asking, Nub was shuddering. Almost involuntarily, Nub glanced back through the door at the shadows that hid things as troubling as what the boy had suggested. A man like Dru's father knew only what he could see and touch, but Nub had learned from his Mescalero mother that the world might be alive with power beyond a cowboy's understanding.

70

"Enough of this — what about the horses?" Jake pressed the *muchacho*. "You bringin' 'em?"

"*Sí, tres caballos.*"

"Three?" repeated Nub.

"My *caballo* too. *El brujo* need to die. Bullets no *buenos*. *Mi papá* taught me how to kill."

With renewed vigor, Alfonso was away, running for the horse trap as even more unanswered questions raced through Nub's mind.

CHAPTER 4

"What have we witnessed?"

For half a mile Nub had run alongside his would-be father-in-law, the two of them bearing west with the raiding party's beaten trail toward the Rim's dark and toothy range. They had left a dead man and more behind, and now Nub and Jake were alone in the long shadows of Spanish daggers, ocotillo, and lechuguilla, a pair of men no better than yapping pups chasing a screaming panther that could devour them in a single bite.

"Inside the store," continued Nub to the pounding of their boots. "In God's name, what have we witnessed?"

Jake huffed as he struggled to match Nub stride for stride. "God didn't have nothin' to do with it."

"The blood," stressed Nub. "What —"

"Since when a Indian ain't seen blood?"

Nub dropped the matter; Jake wasn't in a

frame of mind to discuss it. Not only that, but for a man of Jake's age to sustain a run at this altitude, talking only taxed his lungs more.

But silence couldn't keep Nub from replaying what he had seen. Ever since they had passed the storekeeper's forlorn home — the cross at its nearby mound shining in the sun — the dripping throat and bloody cup had dominated his thoughts, as had Alfonso's troubling words.

And worst of all was what everything might mean for Dru and Ruthie.

Outside the store, Nub had secured the provisions to his belt and reloaded with double-aught buckshot. At a maximum distance of forty yards, the eight .33-caliber pellets in a shell could penetrate deeply across a forty-inch spread. Nub's pump-action Stevens shotgun had its limitations compared to a carbine, but at the right distance it could incapacitate two or three raiders with a single shot.

Whether any of it would make a difference he could only pray.

At least Nub knew where the raiders were headed in the near term. For forty-five miles across the horizon, the Rim was a barrier. A mile and a half ahead through the yucca, its hills pushed up, climbing out of Capote flat to crest at more than a mile above sea level. At Split Peak, four miles from headquarters, awaited an abrupt thousand-foot plunge. And the only way down to the Rio Grande badlands — the only way possible for half a day's ride left or right — would be by an old Apache trail that Nub's mother had told him of traveling.

It was strange how life had come full circle for Nub, the blood son of a warrior. Only because his mother had been abducted by Apaches as a young girl had he even been born. A great wrong had been done to her, and yet because of it, he was here now, pushing through agave and pitaya cacti with Jake, the two of them perhaps the only chance for two other victims of the same kind of injustice.

But a woman seized by Apaches had been safe from outrage, if not death, while the animals who had Dru and Ruthie . . .

Tightening his jaw, Nub wondered what he would do if Jake again shouldered his carbine against them.

How different this Christmas Day was from what Nub had expected: the announcement and the anticipation of sharing with Dru a journey into tomorrow. Instead, it was the darkest day Nub could have imagined, from the first shots to Jake's

74

rudeness to a horde of animals riding off with Ruthie and Dru. *Dru, for God's sake!* And Nub had no control over any of it, except, perhaps, his relationship with her father.

He looked at the aging man who stubbornly tried to keep pace at his shoulder. Blood caked Jake's nose, evidently from a wound he had suffered outside the residence, and it had streamed down and dried in his drooping, gray mustache. He was battle-tested and scarred, but Nub wondered what it would take to chip away at that part of him that wanted nothing to do with Nub.

"I love your daughter, Mr. Graves."

Jake's mustache twitched, but he didn't turn.

"I realize you don't approve," added Nub, "but I love her."

The tic grew worse in the leathery furrows of a cheek burned dark by sun.

"Might you at least respect our feelings for one another?" pressed Nub. "When two people love —"

The older man whirled on him. "You think love's enough? Hell, the things I could tell you. Love can keep you from doin' what you got to sometimes!"

Then Jake asked something that seemed

to confirm what Dru's mother had suggested: that he carried a burden from the past.

"So how is it with you Indians? Why wasn't killin' ever enough?"

"Sir?"

"Here you'd come a-raidin', bunch of filthy Comanches carryin' off some girl. Why wasn't killin' her enough?"

"I . . . Mr. Graves, I'm of Apache heritage. Not Comanche."

"Same damned difference," snorted Jake as he turned away.

They dropped into a catclaw-lined arroyo with two-foot undercut banks, and fifty yards up the narrow wash they stopped at a point where the far bank had sloughed. The rubble was fresh, forming a mound six or seven feet long, and through the crawling dust on top, sunlight shined from a button.

"Throwed him under the bank . . . caved it off," Jake wheezed. "Gold Buttons hisself."

"The uniformed man you dispatched?"

"Least, they didn't leave him for the buzzards like . . ."

There it was again, an apparent allusion to some black memory. But Jake quickly followed up with a statement that Nub wished could be said of every bandit ahead of them.

"That's one devil . . . that'll be havin' . . . Christmas dinner in hell."

The older man could barely find air enough to say the words, and by necessity he lingered at the spot, his chin falling against his heaving chest as he leaned over with a hand on the muzzle of his supporting carbine.

Nub, meanwhile, struck by the sight of another dead man, considered again the blood back at the store.

"When Alfonso first decried Rentería as a *brujo,* I took it metaphorically," he said.

When Jake didn't respond, Nub motioned to the grave.

"Like you christening this man a devil," Nub elaborated. "To you he *is* a devil, but not literally. Alfonso's expression was such that he really believes Rentería is a witch."

Jake looked up, his gray eyes narrowing.

"Listen, boy," he snarled. "They took my daughter and niece 'cause of you. That's all I care about."

"Knowing Rentería's mind-set could be an advantage, Mr. Graves. If we are to rescue —"

"Rescue, hell!" interrupted Jake. "You think that's what this is, a rescue?"

"Sir?"

"We'll find 'em, all right," Jake growled

77

through a wheeze. "And we'll bury what the buzzards . . ."

Dru's father went silent, leaving Nub with a terrible picture in his mind. He hadn't thought the day could turn any more somber, but he had been wrong. It ignited a desperate fire in him, and he knew what he had to do.

Stuffing his pockets with shotgun shells, Nub set the supply sack in the arroyo bed and faced the winded man.

"Sir, sunset is almost on us. It's imperative I get to the Rim and reconnoiter. They may not hold to the old trail after descending on the other side. You should wait here for the horses."

With the advantage of youth and the blood of his Apache forebears, Nub was away in a run, determined to give his all or die trying.

Jake had never felt so old, and he didn't like it.

Considering the places he had been and the things he had done in his sixty-three years, it wasn't right for his body to abandon him when he needed it most. Yet here he was, blowing hard as he slumped on the arroyo bank with his legs draped over the edge, while the worst kind of devils rode farther and farther away with Dru and Ruthie.

Where was the stamina he had once had? It seemed only yesterday that he could do a man's work and ask for more. Now, after running barely half a mile, he was just a shell, one whose will struggled against the realities of his age.

His knees ached. There was pain in his ankle, and he had a catch in his lower back that extended to his hip. He felt weak all over, and the only thing he could do was open a can of tomatoes with his pocketknife and turn it to his lips.

The salty juice helped, and so did the mushy tomatoes.

He hadn't realized how dehydrated he was, but he required a second can just to quench his thirst. His vigor, though, was another matter, and regardless of how much he wanted to push on by foot, his better judgment told him to wait for the horses and trust Nub to reconnoiter.

Trust Nub.

An Indian.

Jake felt every one of his years, all right, and he didn't like it worth a damn.

The distinct shadows of Spanish daggers and ocotillo lengthened more and more and then disappeared as the sun fell behind the sloping uplift of the Rim at his back. Exhausted and discouraged, his head lowered, Jake lost track of time as he sat with his carbine across his thighs and replayed two moments separated by nearly half a century. He was vaguely aware that dusk crept upon him from all sides, but he didn't realize night had fallen until a limb popped from the direction of headquarters.

Jake flinched and stood up in the arroyo. Pivoting, he searched the dark, the rifle barrel at his hip swinging with him.

Silence. A long silence. Then the wind shifted, blowing into his face, and he heard the low drumming of nearing hoofs — too many for the three horses Alfonso had promised. Scrambling up the bank, Jake crouched behind a big yucca's twisted trunk and waited.

Against a three-quarter moon, rising just to the left of the silhouetted cones at the point of Capote Ridge, something moved.

Even as he took a bead on the winking orb, Jake longed for the past morning, when he had waited for the sun to rise from the same spot and his only worry had been about Dru and Nub. How things had changed in these few hours. How he wished to have the day back, to live it again free of a nightmare.

But all he could do was steady his aim and watch as shadow riders came closer.

There were voices in the night, whispers carried on the currents. They were punctuated by the distant *yip-yip* of a coyote, and the hoot of a nearby owl, but the murmurs persisted until Jake could almost make out words. Then the party must have dropped into the arroyo, for hoofs began to crunch gravel. Soon, Jake was in earshot of a conversation in English between two riders and a third who spoke the language haltingly and with a heavy Spanish accent.

Jake took a calculated risk. "Alfonso, that you?"

The moment he called, Jake rushed to a new position — a safeguard against an instinctive shot by friend or foe. As he did, the voices went quiet, and so did the hoofs.

"*¿Quien es?*" someone eventually asked. "*¿Señor* Jake?"

Jake relaxed. "Who you got with you, Alfonso?"

"*Señor* Capps."

"Who?" Jake asked in surprise.

"Bill Ike Capps," answered a gravelly voice. "Me and my boy both."

Jake didn't know if he was glad to see Bill Ike or not, much less his grown son, Bo. Over the years, Jake had come across all

81

kinds of men: honest and crooked, pleasant and disagreeable. Bill Ike was downright mean. More than once, Jake had seen him mistreat an unruly bronc, and anyone who was cruel to horses was a no-account bastard in Jake's book.

"What are you doin' here, Bill Ike?" Jake asked, stepping down into the arroyo.

"Bo here heard the shootin' this mornin'. We come to help."

Jake had his doubts. Bill Ike wasn't any better with people than he was with horses. Residing in a shack off the Valentine road two miles from Cross C headquarters, he was the most unobliging of neighbors, according to Annie's brother-in-law. Maybe Bill Ike's hardscrabble life had shaped his outlook, but who in this country *didn't* face the wolf at the door at times? "Land rich and cash poor" described just about every rancher Jake knew, although his in-laws had done all right with the Cross C's.

Regardless, scratching hard for a living didn't give Bill Ike an excuse for being a jackass set on skinning everybody. Jake himself had exchanged words with him once, and the two men had nearly come to blows.

"We been through hell all day," Jake told him. "You try gettin' the Army boys out?"

"Ain't got no phone. We was leery of showin' ourselves, so we holed up till dark 'fore startin' over for a look-see."

A few feet in front of Jake, the riders stopped, the backlighting moon rendering them silhouettes.

"Alfonso," Jake asked, "you get us some horses and saddles?"

"*Sí, buenos caballos.* Spurs too."

Jake accepted a pair of jingling spurs from Alfonso and buckled them on. After taking up the supply sack, he reached for Alfonso's extended arm and found reins.

"The wetback here says they taken Ruthie."

Jake immediately recognized Bo's nasal voice. The younger Capps was no better a candidate than his father to get involved in somebody else's fight, and the shadows in his face couldn't make Jake forget the dissipation that had taken a physical toll on him. Still in his twenties, Bo already had an alcoholic's nose with its broken blood vessels, and spider veins marked his flushed cheeks. His eyes were always bloodshot and the lids puffy, and even from where Jake stood securing the provisions to the saddle, he could smell the stale alcohol in Bo's sweat and on his breath.

As Jake swung across the saddle, the

liquor had yet another effect. It loosened the young man's tongue at a time that called for self-restraint.

"Graves," Bo added, without the "mister" that Jake's age should have warranted, "you should've stood up to those Meskins."

Jake burned hot as he reined the horse about to face him. "What are you spoutin' off about?"

"I'd've never let them carry Ruthie off."

Jake breathed sharply. "What gives you the right to tell me what I oughta done? She's my own niece, damn it."

"I'm just saying —"

"They got my daughter too. Forty of them devils, just two of us to fight 'em. Don't you be tellin' me nothin'."

That shut Bo up, but Bill Ike jumped to his defense.

"He don't mean to rile you, Graves. He's just uneasy about things, same as you are."

No one could be as uneasy as Jake. He had more worries than he could count, and Annie was one of them.

"You seen anything of my wife?" he asked Bill Ike. "She and the cook was walkin' up the Valentine road for help."

"Must've already passed the turnoff, time we started this way."

Jake lifted his gaze to the west, where the

foothills of the Rim rose ghostly in the moonlight.

"Alfonso, Nub's gone ahead to spy on that bunch. Bring that horse and let's you and me ride."

Jake didn't ask Bill Ike and his son to join them, and he didn't expect it. But Bill Ike spoke up.

"I figure me and my boy will be goin' with you."

Jake turned in the saddle with a creak of leather and stared at Bill Ike's burly form in the muted light. Three riders stood no chance against the bandits, and five not much more, but how could Jake say no, even to men such as these?

They rode, following a switchbacking course up a steep incline littered with loot from the store. More than once, Jake leveled his carbine on manlike figures, only to identify them as big Spanish daggers. Then at the howl of a lobo wolf from behind, he looked back toward headquarters and saw small shadows flitting against the moonrise sky. Suddenly he was in a swarm of the things, darting past almost as close as his hat brim.

"*¡Madre de Dios!*"

"What the hell!"

"Damned bats!"

It happened so fast that Jake didn't know who said what, but as his horse shied, he glimpsed riders ducking and swatting. He buried his face in his mount's neck and the moon went dark, snuffed out by a swirling cloud of the things. It was like being in a dust devil, only this one spoke in a thousand high-pitched squeaks. Blinded, he gigged his horse and the animal jumped forward, and moments later the moon came out again.

"Damned things bit me!" exclaimed Bo, coming up beside him.

Jake couldn't resist throwing a scare into him. "Better hope they ain't got the hydrophobia. They's bad about carryin' it."

"Where'd they get you, boy?" asked Bill Ike as they all pulled rein.

"End of my finger!"

"What you get for swattin' at them," said Jake. "They just wanted by you, is all."

"It's bleeding!" added Bo. "Damned things drawed blood! Bill Ike, he right about rabies?"

Jake had never heard anyone else call his own father by his first name, but nothing about the Cappses would have surprised him.

"Take a swig and get your nerve up, boy," admonished Bill Ike. "Little ol' bat can't

86

hurt you none. Let it bleed out good."

"*¡Ay Dios, no!*" spoke up Alfonso. "The *brujo* Rentería will find us!"

"Rentería?" repeated Bill Ike. "That who taken the Cross C girl?"

"My niece and daughter both, I told you," Jake snapped.

"What's Rentería got to do with a bat bitin' my boy?" followed up Bill Ike.

"He more than a *brujo*!" Alfonso continued. "He is a *tlahuelpuchi*!"

"A *what*?" quizzed Bill Ike.

"*Tlahuelpuchi* smell blood *muy* far," said Alfonso. "Every moon, he drink the blood. Rentería kill my sister *chupado por el brujo.*"

Something cold and clammy seemed to crawl down Jake's spine, and he scanned the dark for he didn't know what.

"What's he talkin' about, Graves?" Bill Ike asked.

Jake didn't have an answer; he was busy fighting a sudden feeling that something was sneaking up on him. Rentería was the one person he would have believed almost anything about, except that he practiced witchcraft, and after seeing Rentería's handiwork in the store, even that didn't seem so far-fetched anymore.

Getting no answer from Jake, Bill Ike turned his attention to Alfonso.

"Hey, you — wet. What's all this jabberin' you doin'?"

"It is so, *señor. Tlahuelpuchi* hunt the blood. He change to animal, maybe a bat, and suck the blood till you die."

"Somebody shut him up!"

Jake turned at Bo's voice. In the moonlight, the younger Capps was pulling from a bottle. If there really was something set on finding blood, Jake figured Bo for the most unlikely of victims. Opening a vein in a *borracho,* a drunk, would be like tapping a barrel of whiskey.

Bo may have wanted to silence any alarming talk, but when he lowered the bottle, it was he who followed up with Alfonso.

"This *tlahuel*-thing. That's crazy talk! You saying that's what bit me?"

Given his reaction, Jake figured Bo didn't think it was so crazy after all.

"No, *señor,*" explained Alfonso. "The bats all dark like shadows. *Tlahuelpuchi* glow like the starlight. When he become bat or turkey or coyote or flea, he glow. It is so, *señor.*"

Jake didn't accept a word of it, of course. The horse beneath him, he could feel, and the cane-like stems of a nearby ocotillo, he could see. There was no questioning the wind that whistled in his ears, or the scent of creosote on the currents. All of Alfonso's talk about things beyond a man's senses was just that — talk.

But it didn't matter what Jake thought. If the *muchacho* believed that Rentería wasn't just a man, maybe Rentería believed it too, and Jake had been a lawman long enough to realize that it paid to learn all he could about an enemy. He had just been too stubborn to agree when Nub had said it.

Jake found Alfonso's slender form astride the horse next to him.

"How come you to think Rentería killed your little sister?" he asked.

"*Mi papá* work for candelilla wax buyer on *río.* He hear bad talk, how Rentería is a *tlahuelpuchi* and drink the blood. Then Rentería and *tres hombres* ride up to *mi familia casa,* our home, and take the flour, the corn and beans too. Mama, she nursing my sister, and Rentería stare at little one. Rentería like puma in the eyes when he stare.

"They go, and Papa scared that Rentería come back for my sister. Papa take the rifle and we go outside to watch. Sun go down, and glowing turkey come up from *río.* It fly over *la casa,* our house, and fly over again. It make the crooked cross in sky over *la casa.* Papa say, 'It *tlahuelpuchi*! Rentería change into turkey! Gun *no bueno* against *tlahuelpuchi*!' So we run into *la casa* and close the door."

Bill Ike gave a disrespectful laugh. "Glowin' turkey, hell. You Meskins is scared of your own shadow."

Alfonso's story sounded no less ridiculous to Jake, but he let the *muchacho* continue.

"Turkey too big to get in *la casa.* Coyote or fox either. Papa scared that *tlahuelpuchi* turn into scorpion and crawl inside, so he stuff blanket under door. We watch for glow, but *tlahuelpuchi* get inside anyway. Maybe he become too little to see. Maybe he become tick."

Bill Ike's mocking persisted. "Turkeys, ticks — what'll this crazy Mex come up with next?"

But Alfonso was not deterred. "*Tlahuelpuchi* spray mist. It look like rain in sun and put me sleep. Papa and Mama too. Then *tlahuelpuchi* change into man and go to my sister. Morning come, *tlahuelpuchi* gone and sister dead, *chupado por el brujo.*"

There was that phrase again, *sucked by the witch.* It was a hell of a story, but Jake wanted to get to the truth behind it.

"Your sister been sick?" he asked. "Children can die quick."

"No, *Señor* Jake. It was Rentería the *tlahuelpuchi.* Day before, my sister *estába bien,* all right. He suck the blood. We find her *muerta,* dead, and she all blue, dark like winter storm come in north."

Cholera — the blue death, thought Jake. In hours it could discolor a victim's skin and kill, just as it had his baby brother back in Mason County.

"Still ain't told me what I want to know," said Jake.

"*¿Qué?*"

"You say your father heard talk. Down on the Rio Grande."

"*Ay Dios, muy* bad. *Mi papá's* family from Tlaxcala. Rentería's too. You know Tlaxcala, *señor?* It way south, to east of Mexico Distrito Federal, what *Americanos* call Mexico City."

Tlaxcala. Jake had heard of the small state. Back in the eighties, hundreds of Tlaxcalans had emigrated north and settled on both sides of the Rio Grande.

"*Muchas* Tlaxcalan families cursed with *tlahuelpuchis,*" Alfonso continued. "Families no tell, but Papa was *amigos* with Rentería's brother. They see each other when the brother bring the candelilla wax. Papa learn truth from him. Rentería drink the blood once month or die. Baby's blood best, but *señorita's* blood also *buena* — maybe why Rentería carry *señoritas* away."

Little of what the *muchacho* had said

91

about Rentería and *tlahuelpuchis* could be true. But what Jake still didn't know was what Rentería believed about himself, for in the store Jake had seen evidence he couldn't dismiss. Before, Jake had been tortured by the thought of Dru and Ruthie being violated, but now there was the possibility that a crazed animal might also intend them for an end too terrible to think about.

Shaken more than ever, Jake urged his horse up the trail.

CHAPTER 5

The tall bandit had yet to look directly at her, but Dru could still see a face of pure evil.

She recognized it in his eyes mainly, dark slits as cold and piercing as a diamondback rattler's. But his skin ailment, too, contributed to her uneasy feeling that she looked at someone who was both more, and less, than a man. Maybe the white splotches around his mouth and nose and across his cheeks weren't signs of leprosy, but the effect was no less repulsive than how she imagined the disease would present itself.

The other bandits called him *capitán,* this animal who gave the orders. With her working knowledge of Spanish, Dru thought of him as Sangre, Blood, for a thin stream of it had run down from the corner of his mouth to his bristled jaw and dried. She supposed he had sustained an injury, for his upper lip was likewise stained.

As soon as the bandits had ushered Dru out of rifle range from Cross C headquarters, rough hands had bound her wrists to her saddle horn. Her bonds were tight, and the more she tried to work her hands free, the deeper the rawhide bit into her skin. Nor had Ruthie escaped the cruel hands, and both girls had ridden similarly restrained up the steep incline.

As Dru gained the uppermost reaches of the Rim at a pass between Split Peak on the left and a two-hundred-foot sister bluff on the right, the riders ahead were bunched and waiting to descend the far side, forcing her handler to hold her dun alongside Ruthie. A stout wind blew up through the gap, tousling the dun's mane, and it stung Dru's eyes as she looked down thousands of feet at a broken, painted desert that looked as if it had been sculpted out of hell. There were hues of red and yellow, brown and gray, all splashed against the barren folds of inhospitable canyons and ridges.

Stretching toward a line of distant crags, it was a forbidding land, a fitting place for men such as these.

Over the dun's ears, Dru could see Sangre wave the bandits on, and she watched the riders drop off one at a time to hug a dangerous trail down along the almost sheer west face of the Rim. Suddenly, Sangre's deadly eyes were on her, and his jaw dropped a little. His face strangely paled as he approached tentatively on his raven-black horse, and Dru averted her vision, for she knew better than to make eye contact with a vicious dog.

She was aware when he drew rein alongside on her left. Still, she avoided his stare until fingers dug into her scalp and twisted her head around.

Dark eyes, as wicked as ever. But now they were troubled, even frightened, as they stayed fixed on her.

"*¡La diablesa!*" he whispered hoarsely.

Dru may have known the word — *she-devil* — but she still couldn't understand.

Then Ruthie, abreast on her right, whimpered and drew Sangre's attention, and Dru found her framed against the spiny agave and dark rocks of the bluff beyond. Ruthie had always been excitable, but Dru had never seen her fall apart this way. From the moment a bandit had accosted them at headquarters, Ruthie had cowered and wept and accepted abduction without resistance. She was still ashen, her golden hair wild in the wind, and all she seemed able to do was hang her head and quietly sob "*No, no, no*" again and again.

Abruptly, Ruthie looked up, and she must have seen this face of pure evil.

"Make him go away!" Ruthie cried. "Dru! Dru! Make him go away!"

She continued to wail hysterically, her eyes wide and her wrenched face almost unrecognizable, and Sangre reined his horse around the dun and took it up before her. He reached for something at his waist, and the dying sun came alive in a .45 automatic sweeping up from a cracked leather holster.

"*¡Basta!* Enough!" he shouted.

Dru could see his blood-caked hand around the checkered walnut grip, and the compact, blued barrel flashing light as the muzzle came to rest inches from her cousin's terrified eyes. The development stripped Ruthie of what little control she had left. Screaming, she fought violently against her bonds and unnerved her horse. Her handler, a short-necked Mexican astride an Appaloosa, was caught unawares, and Ruthie's horse bolted from his control.

"After her!" Sangre shouted. "Shut her up!"

The Mexican gave chase, the dust rising to the cadence of two sets of hoofs.

"Don't let him hurt her!" Dru pleaded.

Dru didn't know where she had found the courage, but hers was the voice that still played between the bluffs as Sangre faced her.

"She's scared!" she told him. "She can't help it!"

Sangre's features grew more troubled, and he turned toward the bunched riders, where the short-necked bandit had overtaken Ruthie. *"¡No le hagas dañola!"* Sangre ordered with a wave of his arm.

With the *capitán's* directive not to harm Ruthie, her handler merely seized the bay's bridle and restrained the animal. Dru took it in with a glance, for Sangre began to study Dru again, and once their eyes met, she couldn't look away. She could make out every blood vessel, jagged rays of red against white. There were the dark, cold irises, as repulsive as a pit viper's, and the even darker pupils that seemed to reach deep inside her, probing but not finding.

They were the eyes of a devil, but they also showed a vulnerability that she couldn't understand.

At last, Sangre turned and rode away, but not without a long look back in seeming awe.

Jesús Rentería was shaken, and he struggled to regain his poise as his midnight-black horse picked its way down the treacherous trail from the Rim.

Tracing switchback after switchback, with a sheer wall at his shoulder one moment and a precipice the next, he didn't dare check the single-file riders behind him. Still, the face of the dark-haired *señorita* stayed powerful in his mind. The hint of a dimple in her chin, the gentle swell of her lips, the play of tresses against a tanned cheek — together they conjured up so many things he wished to forget. But of all her features, only the eyes — dark yet bright and graced by long, raven lashes — served to haunt.

With him through the billowing dust went memories separated by two decades, memories that spoke to him over the strike of hoofs and rattle of saddles. Two faces, different yet the same, lured him past sentineling yucca, around whitewashed outcrops, down rubbly pitches that threw his horse back on its haunches in barely controlled slides. And throughout, the guilt raged, roiling Rentería's stomach and setting him shuddering, a vexing plague that blackened the world more than any dusk should.

And all because he had seen someone he couldn't have.

She may have been a gringo, this *Americana* girl, and fully matured, but the resemblance was uncanny. No one should have looked so much like his sister, and yet this twin followed from only a few positions behind, a she-devil stalking him through his gloom. Meanwhile, he pushed against the saddle horn as he plunged a thousand feet by trail into the badlands, and deeper yet into his personal hell.

By the time dayglow approached its end, the packhorses ahead had already laid a track of spilled plunder down from the summit, and the animals remained bound for the Rio Grande hours away. Once across into Mexico, the band would push on through the night and hole up at daybreak in a hidden canyon so that Rentería might divide the spoils. As always, the men would expect to compete for the *señoritas,* a wolf pack's special reward for allegiance.

But Rentería had no wish to submit the she-devil *La Diablesa* to their wanton desires, nor, by extension, did he want her companion *señorita* harmed. As playthings, he had intended them from the start, although playthings destined for a greater cause. Even sated, he had craved the time that would soon come, when the taste on his lips would be like sweet nectar. Now, though, his sister's features in *La Diablesa* gave him pause, and more.

Rentería suddenly felt a strange summons

from the home of his youth, a set of crumbling adobe walls on the outskirts of a village on the American side of the cane-infested Rio Grande. His sister was there, and she seemed to call him from across the years, from beyond a black gulf that no one could span.

Two miles into the badlands, he came upon a dry arroyo trending left, or south, and he held his black and forced the riders behind to bunch up. The pack animals ahead were pulling away, disappearing in the dust with the majority of his command, and he let the separation grow.

At Rentería's rear were five men and the captives, and he could hear the bandits grumbling as he turned in the saddle. *La Diablesa* was three positions back, a manifestation of he didn't know what in the muted light, and he took a moment to stare before motioning to the men.

"*Tráiganlas,*" he ordered. "Bring them."

Veering into the gravelly arroyo, Rentería yielded to the siren call.

For a hundred yards between modest bluffs, he and the contingent traced out a gentle *S,* and then the arroyo fell sharply through shadowy boulders larger than his boyhood home. As demanding as the trail down from the Rim had been, this was worse, and all Rentería could do was give the black its head and rely on its night vision and innate balance. With the rising bluffs squeezing close, he could hear the rasp of jutting rock against his sombrero as he winced to the slap of mesquites and the strafe of agave spines above his boot.

Negotiating a curving gauntlet a third of a mile long, Rentería dropped three hundred feet and reached the floor of a V-shaped canyon bearing on to the south. Nightfall gripped the rocky depths, but the heights were still in twilight and showed brute-black shapes clinging precariously to slopes too steep to hold them. Rentería didn't like this place; the hovering boulders seemed too much like great *lechuzas,* shape-shifting witch owls, poised to swoop.

Shuddering, he glanced back through the choking dark and wondered if even a *lechuza* would be preferable to the black-haired *señorita* who followed.

As Rentería pushed on for a rendezvous with a far-downstream point on the Rio Grande, he remembered and relived and regretted.

Consuela.

He would never forget her. The bounce of raven tresses against youthful shoulders. Coppery cheeks as unblemished as the coat

101

of a young foal. Her prayerful pose upon receiving first Holy Communion. The cock of her head as she had smiled, and the delight in her face when she had announced the courtship of a nice *muchacho.* Even after all these years, the memories were vivid. But no detail still burned in Rentería's soul as did Consuela's dark eyes, eyes so innocent and trusting and clear — and yet so blind to the evil that had ensued.

No fourteen-year-old sister deserved to endure what she had, and Rentería would live all his life in torment.

Tlaxcalan by heritage and *Americano* by birth, the two of them had grown up in La Mina, a Rio Grande village of barking *perros* and sweat-soaked peons who slaved in cornfields under a pitiless sun. Rentería had been Consuela's senior by two years, and their brother Roberto's by four, and when their father had suffered a crippling injury, the responsibility to watch over her had fallen on Rentería's young shoulders.

He had never regretted it, until the moment in childhood when he had come face-to-face with a curse.

Rentería had heard about it all his sixteen years, this affliction that some Tlaxcalans supposedly carried from birth. Never evident in infancy or young childhood, the scourge lurked in a growing child's soul, unknown even to the victim until a year or two after puberty. Then without warning, the adolescent's soul detached, destined to wander in darkness until he accepted his role as an agent of evil. When the soul rejoined the body, the victim was a *tlahuelpuchi* with a craving that could be quenched in only one way.

Human blood.

It was a terrible tale, as old as the Tlaxcalan mountains, and mothers often repeated it to their children to frighten them into obedience. "*Acostárse,* off to bed!" Rentería's own mother had told him, or *tlahuelpuchi* would drain his blood! The threat had worked, but night after night, Rentería had hidden under the covers and shivered, knowing that even prayers couldn't protect him.

As the years passed, the thought of *tlahuelpuchi* became increasingly disturbing, and by the time Rentería took over his father's role as provider, *tlahuelpuchi* seemed to hide behind every cornstalk as the boy worked the fields, in every pail of water he brought up from the *río,* in every shadow of the night as Consuela and Roberto drifted off to sleep nearby. Ultimately, Rentería lay awake not in fear for himself, but to protect defenseless Consuela from *tlahuelpuchi.*

A fixation had it become, and there was no escaping it.

The onset of puberty only fueled Rentería's obsession, but in a way even more terrifying. Although most *tlahuelpuchis* were female, changes in Rentería's body signaled young manhood and he began to brood that he himself might be a *tlahuelpuchi,* that it was only a matter of time before the curse hiding in his soul would seize him.

"Let it afflict somebody else!" he beseeched *Dios,* the Almighty. "*Por favor, mi Padre!* Just spare me!"

Night after night, Rentería prayed for mercy, and day after day, he awakened in relief to find that he was still a *muchacho* and not something more. By sixteen, he was sure that the window of danger had passed, that his sole fear of *tlahuelpuchi* need be only from the outside, and not from the inside.

And then had come that fateful morning.

Sprawled on the rock summit of the Rim's Split Peak, Nub trained his field glasses on the receding line of riders down and away in the shadowy badlands.

As dusk had crept across the broken country, the bandits had appeared and disappeared with the windings of the Apache trail. The trace had borne the single-file horsemen increasingly farther away, and with nightfall imminent, Nub could no longer distinguish individuals. But earlier, among the eight riders on drag, he had seen the swing of shoulder-length black hair and the toss of blond tresses. Now, as the rear of the march broke away to the left and dropped out of sight, he was confident that the contingent included Dru and Ruthie.

Good Lord, he had to overtake them!

Committing the crossroads to memory, Nub turned and scrambled back toward headquarters in the hope of meeting Jake and Alfonso with the horses. Three times in the span of a quarter mile down the slope, he started to pivot back and continue the chase on foot, and then from out of the low-hanging moon came riders.

There should have been two of them, but Nub counted four silhouettes in the time it took to bring up his shotgun. The riders were upon him quickly, and for an instant he wondered if he would hear their gunshots before he died. Then someone shouted a challenge, and he lowered his weapon in recognition of Jake's voice.

"It's I, Mr. Graves!" Nub rushed forward. "Have you a horse for me?"

The smallest rider met him and passed reins and jingling spurs into his hand. "Horse *bueno, Señor* Nub."

Nub stooped and placed a spur band against the heel of his boot. "Who accompanies you, Mr. Graves?" he asked with a glance up.

Dru's father stayed strangely silent, but a gruff voice spoke up from the back. "Bill Ike Capps. My boy's here with me."

Now it was Nub who went quiet for a moment, but as he buckled the spur strap across the front of his boot, he scanned the moonlit figures for the son.

"What business have you here, Bo?" Nub asked with thinly veiled contempt.

The younger Capps grunted. "That's *Mister* Bo. We's come to help Ruthie."

Bo could have left it at that, but he didn't. "Not that it's any concern," Bo added, "of somebody like you."

Nub knew what he meant: *of a damned Siwash like you.* After all, back in the summer the two men had locked horns, and Bo's memory of it was probably as strong as Nub's. Indeed, Nub relived the incident even as he studied him in the dark.

Where the northernmost foothill knob of Capote Ridge came down to the desert grasslands, a huge, sculpted boulder perched on the yucca slope. Standing less than a mile from headquarters, it marked the unfenced boundary between the Cross C's on the west and the Capps outfit on the east. Nub had found them together there, Ruthie and Bo, and he hadn't liked what he had seen from the stirrups of his horse as he had approached unseen through the ocotillo stalks.

They were sitting in the boulder's shade, and Ruthie was giggling as they passed a flask. Instinct led Nub to hold his roan in the camouflaging shrubs and watch, and the scene grew more concerning. Ruthie was all too free in yielding to Bo's kisses, even as Bo was disturbingly familiar with his hand against her blouse.

Nub's job was to run the Cross C's, not involve himself in family matters. Nevertheless, he felt responsible for Ruthie, more so than for the whole Cross C herd, and he intentionally rattled a dead sotol stalk as he took his horse forward.

"Miss Ruthie," he said.

Startled, both of them spun, Ruthie going red with embarrassment as she tried to hide the flask at her side. But if Bo was embarrassed, no one could have told it from his face, considering the alcoholic flush that always lay across it like a fire.

A few yards shy of the pair, Nub pulled rein. As he stared and the two of them stared back, the silence was like the charged lull between a flash of lightning and the thunder to follow.

"Miss Ruthie," Nub finally said, "I think it's time you returned to headquarters."

Ruthie dropped her gaze and started to rise, but Bo took her arm and prevented it.

"Get out of here, you damned Siwash," he ordered Nub with slurred words.

"It's time, Miss Ruthie," repeated Nub.

Now, the drunken man permitted her to stand, and sunlight glinted in the flask as she handed it to him. Bo rose with her, and as she went to a nearby ocotillo and untied her bay, he mumbled to himself and stumbled back against the boulder.

Ruthie had mounted up and ridden away in silence with Nub. But even on the trail of her abductors on this Christmas night months later, he could still see her disheveled blouse and smell the strong odor of alcohol on her breath.

With both spurs in place, Nub swung up across his horse and wheeled the animal to face Bo.

"I trust," said Nub, "that you intend to maintain sobriety."

Nub couldn't read the younger Capps's

features in the silvery light, but the grunt was unmistakable.

"Always butting in where you don't belong," Bo growled. "You damned —"

"Some kind of stink between you two?"

Jake's stern voice abruptly dominated the night.

" 'Cause if they is," he continued, "I want it settled right here and now. We got things that got to be done."

"It's that foreman causin' the trouble, not my boy," interjected Bill Ike. "Bo's done got bit up by a bat in all of this."

"A bat?" repeated Nub.

"Own fault for tryin' to fight them off," said Jake.

Nub was ready to ride, but Bill Ike wasn't finished. "Graves, this Indian of your brother-in-law's needs to stay in his place."

Jake drew a sharp breath. "I expect Nub will have his say anytime he gets ready."

Surprised, Nub turned, for Dru's father had unaccountably defended him rather than criticized. Nub wanted to let the moment linger, but this was a time to act rather than process what it might mean.

"All that matters is Dru and Miss Ruthie," Nub said. "But we must hurry, Mr. Graves. I reconnoitered from the Rim, and we must hurry."

CHAPTER 6

Off her dun at the canyon bottom, Dru looked up at the horseman moving against the sunrise sky, a burnished figure traversing the high ridge.

Fading into shadow as he zigzagged down the agave-studded slope toward her, the skinny rider with the crooked nose and missing teeth pulled up before Sangre, who stood holding his black horse alongside the other dismounted bandits. For the last ninety minutes of night, they had walked and led the animals, resting them after the brutal ride.

"Cinco," the skinny man reported. "Five riders, a hour behind."

Dru looked back, buoyed for the first time by a glimmer of hope.

Sangre, meanwhile, took the news without a change in expression, but a bandit who stood beside him developed a tic in his pockmarked cheek.

"They're almost as many as us," he said. "Why we not all stay together, *Capitán?*"

"*¿Por que, Capitán?*" agreed a short-necked Mexican. "The packhorses went across the *río.* When we get our share?"

"Or the *señoritas?*" added another man.

"*Sí,* the *senoritas!*"

Five sets of wanting eyes turned to Dru, and to Ruthie at her left shoulder. Shrinking against the fender of the dun's saddle, Dru figured it was just as well that her cousin's knowledge of Spanish was limited. As it was, Ruthie was perpetually ashen, although her voice seemed not to have a whimper left.

Not that Dru was any less frightened, at least in her own way. Worst was the not knowing, the expectancy that at any moment the vilest thing imaginable might happen, and if not at this moment, then the next or the next.

And there would be no one to stop it, not Nub or her father or anyone else who might be following.

"*Por favor,*" persisted the short-necked Mexican. "Where you taking us, *Capitán* Rentería?"

Rentería. Jesús Rentería. So that was the identity of the man whom Dru had thought of as Sangre. She had heard her father mention him repeatedly, but never without revulsion in his voice and a tightening of his jaw. Indeed, she remembered now how her father had called the name from the doorway of the main residence as bandits had seized her horse.

"¿Sí, donde, Capitán?" asked the Mexican who had reconnoitered. "Where are we going?"

As much as Dru had feared Rentería by another name, her dread increased tenfold with the realization of who he was. Even more concerning, he now he looked directly at her. But strangely, judging by his eyes, he seemed almost as afraid of her as she was of him.

"Donde? Where, Capitán?" the scout asked again.

Rentería's troubled gaze stayed on Dru. "Hasta los fines del purgatorio," he whispered. "To the ends of purgatory."

"Que? What?"

But Rentería's attention was on Dru alone. Indeed, his bearing around her was as odd as when they had first faced one another on the Rim.

"Are you señorita or diablo?" he probed with a quake in his voice. "Woman or devil?"

Even when his words faded, his blood-stained lips continued to tremble, as if in fearful anticipation of her response. But Dru didn't know what to say.

"Why . . . Why do you ask such a thing?" she managed.

"A *diablo* sent to punish?" he pressed. Then his voice rose, even as his eyes pleaded rather than demanded. "Tell me!"

But Dru couldn't reply to what she didn't understand. "It's you that's been saying it. Yesterday on the Rim, it was you that said I was *diablesa,* a she-devil."

It was neither an acknowledgment nor a denial, but Rentería reacted as if she had confirmed some deeply held fear. He staggered back, his face blanching as much as his diseased skin would allow.

"*Madre de Dios,* go back! Take your evil back to *infierno*! Or . . . Or are you already there? Both of us in hellfire?"

Rentería checked left and right, stricken by obvious panic. Dru turned with him, tracing the rapid eye movement of a man frantically searching for something that he seemed terrified might be there. Maybe he looked for fire. Maybe he looked for brimstone. Perhaps, even, he saw both with his mind's eye. As he faced her again, all Dru knew was that she and Ruthie were in the clutches of a madman.

"What do you want from me?" he asked.

Dru could only stare at him.

"*Por favor,* you must tell me!" he begged.

Dru glanced at her cousin, and beyond her at the way they had come from up-canyon. "Just let me go home. Both of us."

Rentería's dark eyes had gone wider with every passing second, and now they stayed fixed on her as he silently mouthed a word. Dru could almost make it out, three syllables that played on his lips until he whispered it.

"Consuela!"

For a moment, Rentería looked at Dru in seeming awe, and then he added something that gave her true hope.

"*Sí,* I . . . I'm taking you there! *Muy pronto,* I'm already taking you home!"

With a bone-handled knife, he cut the girls' bonds. But once Dru and her cousin were astride their horses, riders took positions in front and back and Rentería led the band southward down the canyon — farther and farther away from Marfa and the Cross C's.

Teased and denied, Dru rode on, rubbing her chafed wrists as the horses navigated an unforgiving course through her own personal purgatory. Indeed, it had the look of a place of suffering, a widening gorge cursed by thirst where tasajillo and blind prickly pear vied with agave lechuguilla and pitaya between bone-white rocks. There were so many species of cacti with *devil* in the name — devil's head, devil's claw, devil cholla — that Dru wished she hadn't learned so much from her father. Devil-horned lizards that crept like imps among the rocks added to her sensation that this was less a canyon than a trench in deepest perdition.

"How come he's scared of you?"

Ruthie rode along a few paces ahead, her bay swishing its tail as she twisted around in the saddle. Although her voice was muted, it was the first coherent thing she had said since their abduction, even though her features still showed a pallor that only the dead should have.

"How come, Dru?"

All Dru knew to do was to give a slight shake of her head.

"You speak Mex good," Ruthie went on. "What's he been sayin'?"

"Keep your voice down." Dru checked the front of the march and found Rentería still facing forward. "He doesn't act right."

"How you mean?"

"*Loco.* Like the one-eyed horse Nub told us about, the one always seeing snakes."

Ruthie glanced at Rentería. "What is it *he* sees?"

"Familiar spirits and such, the way he talks. Like in the Bible. He looks at me and goes to talking that way."

Ruthie shuddered. "Mama says familiar spirits are up and down the river, what with the war goin' on. She says that's why there's so much killin' and all."

"Maybe," Dru half agreed. "Some people are evil enough on their own."

"But he *is* scared of you, ain't he?"

"I don't know. He acts it. He's given in to what I asked a time or two. I even thought he was turning us loose, but he didn't."

"What's goin' to become of us?" Ruthie's top eyelids went up and her eyebrows drew together. Whirling, she looked up and down the line of march. "These filthy men! You see the way they look at us?"

"Don't give up, Ruthie. I think there might be help coming. There's five —"

"These animals will take us, Dru. Oh God, they'll do it!"

"Not so loud!" whispered Dru.

Full-fledged panic now showed again in Ruthie's parted lips and in the fallen corners of her mouth.

"Dru! We got to do somethin'!"

Ruthie pulled her bay out of the march and wheeled it back up-trail. The strewn rocks limited a horse's gait, but when she slapped her legs against her mount's ribs, the hoofs reached out. In moments the bay achieved a semblance of a gallop as wild as Ruthie's whipping tresses.

To shouts in Spanish, Dru reined her horse about so she could see her cousin's flight. Even before a bandit turned his mount after Ruthie, disaster seemed inevitable. The young woman's bay lost stride in the lechuguilla clumps and then regained it, the hoofs thrashing the twenty-inch daggers and their hardened tips.

For fifty yards, the animal maintained a stumbling run before it dropped to its knees. For a moment, time seemed suspended, Ruthie's boots still in the stirrups, and then she flew over the bay's head.

"Ruthie!"

Dru's exclamation was lost in the furor around her, but her cousin's cry was clear. Somersaulting side by side with the bay, Ruthie avoided the animal's crushing sinew but couldn't escape the lechuguilla.

Already, Dru had urged the dun after her. Closing, Dru saw the bay scramble up, oozing red, but Ruthie was still sprawled on her side when Dru pulled rein nearby.

Dismounting, she blurted a quick "Are you hurt?" and waded through the spines, her boot uppers protecting her legs. In response, her cousin only moaned, her disheveled hair hiding her face. Blood showed in her torn sleeve, and there was a puncture wound in her hand as she stirred.

"Ruthie! Don't move! You're in shin-daggers!"

For sure, they were all around, some of the toxic points still penetrating. Dru freed her from those she could see, but even when Ruthie turned and stretched out an arm, Dru didn't have the leverage to pull her up.

Then, surprisingly, a brown hand on Dru's right reached down and helped drag Ruthie to her feet, and when Dru turned she found Rentería's leprous-like face with its strange fear.

"See how I help you, Consuela?" he asked, his eyes begging for her favor. "Now I take you and your *amiga* home. Maybe I show you to our brother on the way."

"Home?" repeated Dru. "Please!"

"*Sí,* to Roberto's and on to the *río's* waters." Rentería looked back in the direction from which they had come. "And nobody will stop me."

In the trail through the agave lechuguilla, Jake read a story.

Veering from the bandits' south-trending track, it bore back up-canyon, a fifty-yard

118

swath cut by hoofs at a breakneck pace, and from its start to its sudden end at crushed daggers spotted with blood, it spoke of a desperate attempt to escape.

"Somebody got themselves hurt," pronounced Bill Ike.

Leaning off the side of his muscled Appaloosa, Jake had traced the entire course, and now he was back with the other riders at the freshly turned rocks and beaten agave. Only Nub had dismounted, and while Bill Ike rattled on from astride a stocking-footed bay, the young foreman knelt at a lechuguilla clump in inspection.

"Got a cactus under his saddle and headed for Jericho, that bronc did," said Bill Ike, scratching a grizzled goatee that looked lice-infested. "I'd've made the clabberhead straighten up, like my boy done with that spooky roan he's a-ridin'. 'Fore I'd let a horse get me all cut up, I'd've spurred him in the shoulders and took my quirt handle to his head."

All too smugly for Jake's tastes, Bill Ike scanned the other riders, as if ready to accept acknowledgment of his insight. Jake wondered if everyone else realized the know-it-all didn't know a damned thing.

Still, Jake wished that someone, even Bill Ike, could tell him whose blood — Dru's or

Ruthie's — blighted the lechuguilla spines. It was left to Bo to broach the matter.

"You think it was Ruthie got hurt, Bill Ike?" he asked his father. The spider veins and alcoholic flush across Bo's cheeks were on full display in the morning sunlight. "She needs somebody to look after her."

"She'd do well with you, boy," said Bill Ike. "Couldn't do any damned better."

Like hell, thought Jake. Staring at father and son, he found himself gripping the saddle horn so tightly his hand hurt.

But a glare couldn't deter Bill Ike from blathering more to Bo. "I expect she'll be awful grateful, you ridin' after her this way," said the older man.

"I'm hoping her folks will be too," said Bo.

Jake looked at Nub, who was still down on a knee at a bent lechuguilla clump. At first, the foreman's back was turned, but considering the raised upper lip as Nub twisted around, Jake could tell that neither of them wanted this drunkard anywhere near Ruthie.

Jake's instinct was to set Bo straight, but this wasn't the time. The girls were ahead somewhere. They were vulnerable and frightened, under constant threat if not already hurt and bleeding. Still, Jake found

120

himself throwing another scare into Bo.

"If I was you, I'd worry less about gainin' my niece's favor and more about comin' down with the hydrophobia."

Bo's cheek twitched, his skin paling. He quickly checked his finger and addressed his father.

"He's not right, is he, Bill Ike? The bite's just a pinprick. You told me —"

"Aw, hell," said the elder Capps. "You done washed it good with whiskey."

"That good enough? You think that killed it out, Bill Ike?"

"Listen, boy, soon's you catch up with that sweet little girl of yours, you won't be worried about nothin' but you and her and all that Cross C country."

Jake's temple began to pound. What the hell was going on? Ruthie, involved with this sorry excuse for a man?

"Rabies constitutes a grave threat," spoke up Nub. "Once symptoms manifest themselves, the disease is invariably fatal."

Jake didn't know if Nub had intended to frighten Bo more, but the latter's bloodshot eyes went wider, highlighting the dark circles underneath.

"Can't anything be done?" asked Bo. "Can't a doctor do something? I've got to get help, Bill Ike!"

Damn, thought Jake. He hadn't meant to alarm Bo to the point of him giving up the chase. No matter their motives, at least the Cappses were here, balancing out the odds in the fight that was sure to come when they overtook the Mexicans.

Fortunately, Nub stood up with advice for Bo. "It would serve you well to maintain your poise. The incubation period generally exceeds a month."

"See, boy?" said Bill Ike. "Quit your worryin'. Plenty of time for ridin' and fightin' and courtin'."

Jake clutched the saddle horn even more firmly. Didn't either of the girls have a lick of sense when it came to men?

Then Nub held up his blood-smeared fingers and focused Jake's attention on all that mattered for now.

"It abides wet to the touch," said the foreman, making his way to a waiting sorrel. "The riders precede us by no more than an hour. We need to ride, and do so quickly."

"*¡Ay Dios!*" exclaimed Alfonso from his chestnut. "Blood-smell do things to *tlahuelpuchi.* If Rentería no drink the blood this month, he on fire with the fever."

Even as Nub stepped up on his horse, he turned with a confused crease between his eyebrows.

"You missed Alfonso's tellin', back over the Rim," Jake grunted. Carbine in hand, he glanced down-canyon, anxious to push on.

"Silliest damned thing you ever heard, all them windies of that Mex's," added Bill Ike. "Glowin' turkeys, hell!"

"Rentería more than a *brujo, Señor* Nub," explained Alfonso. "He a *tlahuelpuchi. Mi papá* learn it so from Rentería's *hermano,* brother. You *sabe tlahuelpuchi?* I tell you long time ago."

Just before they took up the chase again, Nub looked at Jake and Jake looked back, aware that the younger man shared his troubling memory of Capote Store.

On into midmorning, Jake rode without pause, rolling smoke after smoke and searching the distance for a dust plume that wasn't there. After a quick stop for tomatoes, he and the others forged ahead, walking and leading the tired horses. As the minutes wore on, the march lengthened out, with the Cappses on point, Alfonso in the middle, and Jake hobbling along on drag behind Nub and his sorrel. Jake had napped in the saddle, and the tomato juice had revived him a little, but his knee ached like hell as he watched the sorrel's back hoofs plod through creosote shrubbery and prickly cholla.

" 'There are more things in heaven and earth than are dreamt of.' "

At Nub's voice, Jake lifted his gaze and found the foreman looking back at him.

"It's from Shakespeare," Nub added, "something I learned from my mentor on the Singing Waters outfit. It's a powerful reminder of what my mother told me about the Sierra Diablo, the events in 1881 that led to our lives being changed."

Changed, hell, thought Jake, his old Ranger blood running hot. The important thing about that final Indian fight in Texas had been the white lives *saved* by the Rangers' punitive strike.

"You Mescaleros was raidin' right and left," he said bitterly, remembering another tribe, another place. "Rangers had to do somethin', and they damned sure put a stop to it."

"Be that as it may, my mother remains convinced that the transgressions of a warrior-witch brought about the defeat of her people."

"You mean *your* people," Jake growled. "You was right in the thick of it."

"A child of mere months in a cradle-board."

"So what's this got to do with anything?"

As Nub stopped and faced him, the foreman looked more Indian than ever — the drooping nose, the prominent cheekbones, the coppery cast to his skin.

"I can no more rule out that Rentería is a *tlahuelpuchi*," said Nub, "than I can dismiss my mother's claim that witchery led to the defeat in the Diablos."

Jake went quiet, studying his eyes.

"If he *is* a *tlahuelpuchi*," Nub continued, "we must bear in mind he may have abilities we cannot perceive."

Despite his disbelief in such things, Jake felt the hairs rise on the back of his neck.

CHAPTER 7

As Rentería rode, he carved on a small section of wood he had hacked from the limber branch of a shrubby *tornillo.*

It had multiple forks and numerous thorns, this cutting from what gringos called a screwbean, and maybe he should have thought of it by its gringo term, considering his intent and the *Americanos* who followed. The wicked barbs demanded caution, and he sliced them off before setting about to shape the cutting the way his mind pictured. Chips flew over his black's mane as he whittled and gouged, and although the horse's gait wasn't favorable to fine craftsmanship, a tiny figure began to emerge.

As he contemplated his handiwork, the years seemed to roll back, and Rentería relived as vividly as yesterday that fateful awakening when life had changed forever.

Sharing a pallet with his young brother Roberto in the home of their youth, Rentería had opened his eyes at sunrise to find the world drifting away — the floor under his blankets no longer supporting, the adobe walls and sunlit window receding, the snoring of their disabled father and the braying of a donkey fading to silence. Then a strange dark settled over sixteen-year-old Rentería, a cold, suffocating night even though it was day, and as the gloom lingered, he was certain that it would last forever.

But in a pinpoint of light growing larger, he saw Consuela, sweet Consuela, and she ignited in him a fire he couldn't understand.

The inexplicable dark went away, but his unquenchable thirst grew stronger for something he couldn't identify. Before, his obsession had revolved around *tlahuelpuchi,* but now he was transfixed by his sister. As the sun crept across the sky and a full moon followed in its wake, Rentería stared at her — stared while she shucked corn and boiled it in the adjacent lean-to, stared as she washed clothes in the *río* and slapped them against the white boulders to dry, stared as she drifted off to sleep in blissful ignorance.

Bewildered into the next sunrise, young Rentería retreated with a whetstone to the riverbank and sharpened his knife to a fine edge. He honed it until it shined like the sun in the rippling waters. For the moment, his knife ruled his every thought, although he had no idea why. Rasping his thumb along the edge, the blade drew blood, hot red blood that was sweet against his tongue. And suddenly he had known what must be done.

"Ruthie!"

Startled back into 1917, Rentería wheeled his mount to see the blond *señorita* slide down the shoulder of her horse and collapse under its breast. Consuela's devil twin was dismounting alongside, still calling her name, and by the time Rentería took his animal back up the column, this black-haired manifestation of his sister hovered over the fallen *señorita.*

"*¿Que pasó?*" Rentería asked, finding the two framed in the arch of the bay's neck and head. "What's wrong, Consuela?"

She pressed her hand to her *amiga's* forehead. "She's burning up with fever!" she said without turning. "Ruthie? Ruthie?"

She asked more things of the unconscious *señorita,* but Rentería's knowledge of English was limited. Regardless, he recognized the puncture wounds in the inflamed face, along with the dark stains in her clothes, and he knew that whatever ill effects the horse wreck had failed to inflict, the poison-tipped daggers had managed.

Rentería called for one of his men to bring a can of tomatoes, and soon the devil twin supported her *amiga's* shoulders and tilted the can to the swollen lips. As Rentería watched up-canyon, he allowed the *señorita* more minutes to recover than they could risk, but finally she was able to be helped into the saddle. Still, she slumped over the horn, a pitiful rider cherished by the thing that was Consuela, and yet which could not be Consuela.

Rentería knew they had to push on, but the black-haired one spoke to him from the dun that may have spirited her from *infierno.*

"She needs help. You've got to get her help."

The eyes, dark and bewitching. Just as on that baffling day of his awakening.

In an instant, he was back in that moment, a boy of sixteen whose strange fever raged like the bloated afternoon sun. He had left twelve-year-old Roberto in the fields and fled sweaty and dirt-caked, but as Rentería stepped inside the shielding *la casa,* his affliction grew only worse — for Consuela was there, dabbing their father's beaded face with a cotton cloth.

Her delicate fingers . . . her soothing words . . . the soft, white flesh in her stately

129

neck. She dominated Rentería's thoughts as never before, and he was displeased when the nice *muchacho* from the *pueblo* called on her and she joined him outside. Still, from the shadows inside the door, Rentería kept his gaze on his sister until the *muchacho* led her away upriver.

Lost in budding love, neither Consuela nor her suitor realized that Rentería followed. He trailed them past stands of tall cane and through saltbush and cholla, around screwbean chaparral and lacy-leafed mesquites, and on to a small clearing that ended at a drooping black willow that shaded the west sun.

Kneeling behind a concealing catclaw, Rentería watched through the gray-green leaves as the two of them stood holding hands. For an hour Rentería watched, listening to her gay laughter and studying the smile that showed her white teeth. Then the *muchacho* stole a quick kiss and they parted, the young man striking out upriver while Consuela turned for home.

A part of Rentería that he didn't recognize waited for her, thirsting as never before for what she alone seemed to offer, and abruptly she was before him, ready to fulfill his terrible need.

"We've got to do something for her!"

The voice of Consuela who couldn't be Consuela pulled Rentería back into 1917 once more, and he knew he must appease this visitation who tested him in this grim place of lechuguilla and pitaya, ocotillo and screwbean. Turning his gaze down-canyon to a distant stand of giant yucca, he pondered the trackless way beyond and remembered.

"*Sí, socorro.* We must get your *amiga* help."

Taking his knife afresh to the wood figure, Rentería led them onward into a past that would never let him escape. Indeed, he continued to relive the loathsome deed he had perpetrated at sixteen, and the aftermath when he had wailed his grief over Consuela's body, a ghastly sight under the catclaw.

There had been discoloration, a lot of it, staining his knife and her throat, covering her blouse, darkening the ground. The taste lingered on young Rentería's lips, even as he drew her lifeless form close and wet her hair with his tears.

He wanted to die. But the thing inside him wanted to live, and so Rentería ran back toward the village, only to come upon his ashen brother from behind.

"*¿Dónde has estado,* Roberto?" Rentería

demanded. "Where have you been?"

But Roberto was too shaken to answer, and Rentería seized his brother's arm and the two raced on to the village, where Rentería reported that he had found Consuela murdered in the most horrible of ways. To deflect suspicion from himself, he added that he had seen Consuela's suitor flee the scene, a dripping blade in his hand.

With Roberto too distraught to speak, the search was quick, the punishment swift, the end certain. Villagers hanged Consuela's suitor from a big cottonwood and left the corpse twisting in place for the buzzards.

Once a month thereafter, Rentería went looking for a victim that he believed would keep him alive. But he killed much more discreetly now, wandering the villages up and down the river, venturing into Mexico, avoiding taking a life in the same area too frequently. He always returned home to work the fields, even as he sensed that his younger brother knew that he was a *tlahuelpuchi.* If there was comfort to be had, Rentería found it in realizing that Roberto knew the stories of *tlahuelpuchi* as well as he did. Indeed, it was said that if a family member who had yet to reach puberty revealed a *tlahuelpuchi,* he too might fall prey to the curse.

Even so, Roberto never looked at him the same after Consuela's death. There was disquiet in the boy's eyes, and it grew until Rentería could no longer face him. Eventually, Rentería went out one morning, ostensibly to work the fields, and never came back. A few weeks later he was a soldier, destined to rise in the ranks by means of his iron hand.

And with him had gone the black thing that controlled him — *tlahuelpuchi* or demon or just a demented corner of his mind.

Sí, innocent Consuela had been too trusting, and Rentería still lived every moment in regret on this December morning in 1917.

Honing his wood carving on into noon, he took a moment to admire the exaggerated arms and legs of what was now the effigy of a man. Only a single step in the process remained, and he whispered unholy things over his handiwork as he let his black carry him blindly ahead.

Although the defining bluffs had drifted dramatically apart over the miles, the canyon drainage descended only gradually. But when Rentería's horse stopped in a sudden updraft, he looked down along the ruffled mane and found himself on the brink of an almost sheer drop of two hundred feet.

Alarmed, he backed his animal away and looked out across a desert that unfurled between craggy ranges three miles apart. The forbidding landscape was marked by several rock spires, grotesque formations that stood like hellhounds on guard.

On his left, a rubbly game trail descended, and it held enough promise for Rentería to take his black closer. The tracks of wild burros showed in the chalky spoor, ample encouragement to turn the horse down it.

But before he did, Rentería recognized the potential of this place and, with a final whisper, tossed the effigy over the cliff's edge.

When the six bandits and the women had broken away from the main column the previous dusk, Nub had found hope. Now, as the sun burned high over the canyon, discouragement replaced optimism.

It was true that Nub no longer tracked a small army, but instead a pack of wolf's heads that the riders around him could almost match in numbers if not in firepower. Nevertheless, all he could think about were Alfonso's words.

Rentería, a *tlahuelpuchi.*

Nub's intellect whispered the foolishness

of the idea, but the voices of his Apache forebears spoke powerfully, eroding his confidence, crushing the promise of all his tomorrows. He remembered what Dru's father had said — that this was not a mission of rescue, but of recovery and burial — and he turned and glared at this napping man whose bowed head nodded to the gentle rock of his Appaloosa.

Damn him. Damn anyone who would put an image of Dru's grave in a person's mind.

But if Nub accepted what was said about a *tlahuelpuchi,* he and Dru might soon be united in a way that neither her father nor anyone else could prevent.

Early afternoon brought Nub abreast of Jake's Appaloosa at a windswept overlook where the bleached ground fell away sharply, a long and deadly drop to a land of hoodoos and giant daggers. Nub searched in vain for a column of dust, but a few yards to his left, opposite the older man, a trail with recent hoofprints angled downward.

"Hell of a ride them Meskins got us on, boy." From behind, Bill Ike addressed his son. "Expect that girl of yours is worth it, though." Then Bill Ike's voice rose. "Hey, foreman! How much deeded land the Cross C's got these days?"

Nub knew to the acre, and the extent of

the leased range as well, but he didn't pay the grafting old reprobate the courtesy of even a glance.

The social cue of Nub's silence must have been above Bill Ike's perception. "It'd be nice if my boy would cut out a section or two for his ol' daddy," Bill Ike added with a throaty chuckle. "Little bunch of them blooded Herefords too, while he's at it."

"She's a fine one, Ruthie is," said Bo, his words more slurred than usual. "I marry into the family, I imagine she'll see to it you's done right by, Bill Ike."

Courting was one thing, but marrying was another matter entirely, as Nub well knew, and he resisted an impulse to glance over his shoulder at the Cappses. What bothered him most was the way they openly discussed gaining a slice of the Cross C's when Ruthie's life was so much in doubt.

"Hell of a nerve they got."

Drawing Nub's attention to his profile, Jake kept his gaze on the lowlands as he growled the remark under his breath. But there was nothing restrained about his wincing cheek or the deepening scoring at the eye shaded by his hat brim.

"Mr. Graves," said Nub, knowing he would be overheard, "do we presume Miss Ruthie and her parents have abdicated all

136

say in the matter of her matrimony?"

From behind, Bill Ike snorted. But it was Bo, no doubt emboldened by liquor, who spoke up.

"Soon's we get Ruthie home, she rests up a little, I know right where I'm taking her to ask her to marry me," he said defiantly. " 'Twixt our place and the Cross C's, that boulder perched on the first foothill there under Capote. Hey, foreman! You know the place, don't you?"

Now it was Nub who felt his cheek twitch. Bo clearly was baiting him with this reminder of their confrontation, and there wasn't a prudent thing Nub could do about it.

"Said, 'foreman!' " Bo repeated. "Hey, I'm talking to you, Indian!"

Meanwhile, Jake continued to face straight ahead, but his words were directed to the riders behind.

"I said last night, if they's somethin' between you two, it better got settled already. Damned sure not standin' for none of this."

Without waiting for a response, Jake brushed his horse past the nose of Nub's sorrel and took the chalky trail down. As the older man disappeared over the rim, Nub stayed in place, letting Bill Ike proceed next, followed by Alfonso and then Bo. Bo was taking a nip again, even as he kept too tight a rein on the spirited roan with the blazed face, and Nub felt compelled to warn him despite their differences.

"Your animal's markedly nervous. You should allow him his head."

Indeed, the roan's ears were rigid, its eyes wide, and its lower lip tight. Nevertheless, Bo flashed the kind of look he had displayed when Nub had found him with Ruthie.

"I ask any advice from the likes of you?" Bo demanded as he passed. In obvious spite, he took a firmer grip on the reins.

With a disgusted shake of his head, Nub turned his horse into the trail and traced its sharp angle down to the right. He dropped quickly under the rim in bearing for a switchback that avoided a sheer drop ahead, where a slickrock pour-off came down from the dry arroyo on the summit. Already, Dru's father had zigzagged down to the trail's next level, and Nub watched as Bill Ike's bay and then Alfonso's chestnut navigated the switchback in Jake's wake.

Bo was drawing from the bottle again, inattentive and still overbearing with the reins despite his horse's growing restlessness. Before disaster erupted, Nub saw it coming, a tightness in the animal's back that changed into a hump so quickly that there wasn't time to try again to urge Bo to caution. The roan elevated almost in place, jerking its head down between its knees despite Bo's hold and then striking the ground on all-but-stiff forelegs.

The deadly rodeo was on, the rear hoofs repeatedly kicking to the sky as the crazed animal pitched down the trail. Bo shouted in alarm and pulled leather, but the gravel continued to fly as he slammed into the bluff at his shoulder. Just shy of the switchback, a protruding gnarled root peeled him from the saddle, and Bo was down.

For an instant, Nub lost sight of him in the threshing hoofs, and then momentum carried Bo past the switchback and off into the pour-off.

"Hyahhh!"

Reacting with instinct, Nub took his horse recklessly ahead. He gained the switchback as the riderless roan swung left and downward, the stirrups flopping wildly as the animal held to the dog-legged trail. But Nub's focus was on the sharp drop at his own horse's breast, and his loud cry for Bo rolled all the way to the depths. When it echoed back, there was a desperate shriek with it.

"Help me! For God's sake, help me!"

Nub glimpsed movement over the edge, and in moments he was off his sorrel and kneeling at the drop-off. Several feet down, Bo clung to a gnarled scrub mesquite, his arm hooked over the trunk that twisted horizontally out of a sheer wall. With his free hand Bo scratched at the rock face between them, but it was like polished glass.

Lord Almighty!

With Bo's struggles the trunk groaned and gave at its base, dislodging rubble that plummeted past his kicking boots and bounced off a jutting rock a dozen feet farther down. Against the terrifying backdrop of boulders almost two hundred feet below, Bo's face was a mask of panic, his eyes bulging and his mouth agape.

"Help me! You got to help me!" he screamed.

Maybe Nub should have reached for the rope coiled on his sorrel's saddle, but there didn't seem time. Sprawling prone, he extended his arm toward Bo, but the distance was too great. He scooted forward until the cliff edge bit into his chest and his balance was precarious, but Bo was still a foot and a half too far below.

"You must do your part!" Nub shouted. "Reach for me!"

But as the mesquite gave more and more,

Bo only screamed and clawed and kicked, and when he finally stretched out a hand and clasped Nub's, he yanked with terrible force. Suddenly Bo was dragging him to his death, the sharp edge scraping Nub's ribs, and there was nothing Nub could do except let the inevitable happen.

Then something seized Nub's legs and arrested his slide, but he continued to totter on the brink of eternity until Bo planted a knee on the trunk. For anxious seconds there was still a question of whether either of them would get out of this alive, but with Nub's help, Bo managed to scramble to the summit.

The two of them lay there, Nub's arm aching and his lungs heaving as Bo's alcohol-laced sweat hung heavy in the air. Only now did Nub realize that Alfonso stood over him, an outline blazed in the sky, and he understood now that it had been the *muchacho* who had saved their lives.

"*¿Estas bien, Señor* Nub?" asked the excited youth. "You all right? *¿Estas bien?*"

With an arm against his aching ribs, Nub slowly gained his feet.

"*Sí, estoy bien,*" he said with labored breath. Then he placed a hand on the slender *muchacho's* shoulder. "*Gracias,* Alfonso. You're *mucho hombre.* Indeed, *mu-*

cho, mucho hombre."

As Nub turned, he found Bo still writhing and fighting for air alongside the drop-off. On the face of that cliff, there had been a bond in their mutual clasp, and even when things had been grimmest, Nub had never considered wriggling out of Bo's hold. Now, Nub extended another helping arm.

Bo slapped it away. "Get your hand out of my face, you damned Siwash."

In utter disbelief, Nub stared at him.

"That greasy Meskin's too," Bo added, struggling to his feet.

As Bo stumbled away, Nub shook his head and looked down at the pour-off where moments before they had faced death together. From this angle, he saw something on the rock that jutted from the wall below the mesquite, and he edged closer for a better look.

Through the bare, thorny limbs that swayed in an updraft, he made out a small wood carving of a man, its finish testifying to its recent fashioning.

With a shudder, the part of Nub that believed in Apache spirits recognized a *tlahuelpuchi's* voodoo effigy that had drawn two men so close to their end.

CHAPTER 8

"We must be on our guard," Nub warned under the afternoon sun.

He rode abreast of Dru's father as the five struck out across the yucca flat that stretched south from the base of the escarpment. Past the nodding head of Nub's sorrel, the bandits' fresh tracks snaked onward through pitaya and cholla and across dormant spiderling and devil weed. But it wasn't the desert growth that gave him pause, or even the monstrous hoodoos that hovered like harbingers of evil. These were things of substance that could be avoided, but there was no ready defense against powers arising from agents of *el diablo.*

When Nub faced Jake, he found that his warning had drawn the older man's attention.

"There may be things incorporeal that aren't subject to our weaponry," Nub added.

Jake's jaw tightened. "More of your Indian

nonsense?"

"Belief in a spirit world pervades all cultures," defended Nub. "My parents raised me to believe in Christ and His Father. If there's a God abiding in Heaven, there's a devil ruling hell."

A lot of pain seemed to fill Jake's eyes, and his gaze dropped. "Hell's somethin' you can't tell me nothin' about that I don't already know."

Nub wondered if this was the time to broach a matter that had concerned him.

"Mrs. Graves implied at headquarters that you carry a burden from your youth."

Jake looked at him.

"In the context of her remark," Nub continued, "the millstone about your neck influenced your attempt to . . . to . . ."

Nub saw it again: Dru and Ruthie down the barrel of Jake's Marlin carbine.

The older man took a sharp breath. "If I want you to know somethin', I'll tell it myself."

Distress stayed in Jake's face, and Nub regretted that he had pried. As an uncomfortable silence ensued, he all but forgot what he had intended to say about the incorporeal, and then Dru's father reminded him.

"So what is it that's got your Indian feathers so ruffled?"

Nub was relieved the subject had changed. "Are you familiar with voodoo practices, the employment of a doll to inflict harm on someone from a distance?"

"Doll, hell. Little girl play-pretties." Jake patted the stock of the carbine in an angling scabbard under his thigh. "This is a man's way of doin'."

"On a ledge below that mesquite, I saw a newly carved effigy of a man."

"A what?"

"A likeness, a representation. It strains credulity to believe it's mere coincidence."

"So you's tellin' me that Capps boy went off of that cliff 'cause of some doll? Hell, didn't you see the tasajillo stalk he pulled out from under his saddle when we got to bottom? That bronc of his broke in two 'cause he was bein' stuck, not 'cause of some magic doll."

"Perhaps," Nub admitted. "Or else there are —"

"God A'mighty," interrupted Jake, "thought you had more sense than that."

"All I'm contending is that perhaps we should prepare for the unexpected if we are to bring Dru and Miss Ruthie back."

A scowl came over the older man's face. "Can't you pay my girl the same respect you do my niece?"

"Sir?"

"How come is it you put a 'Miss' before 'Ruthie' and you don't for Dru?"

"Mr. Graves, I respect your daughter above anyone I've ever known. It was she who asked that I call her Dru."

Jake grunted. "She shouldn't oughta did that. In this country, we got one place for white people, and we got another for Mexes, and the two ain't to be mixed. Same goes for Indians."

"Even one whose father, for all intents and purposes, is a white man, a former Ranger like yourself?"

Jake grunted again, and Nub continued.

"I didn't choose the lot to which I was born, Mr. Graves. How is heritage the measure of a man?" He glanced over his shoulder at the two men out of earshot on drag. "If that were the case, then you should approve of the younger Capps for Miss Ruthie. He's as white as you, yet your resistance to their prospective union is obvious."

Jake's cheek twitched. "I'd partner up with a snake 'fore I'd shake on a deal with Bill Ike Capps. Same goes for his son. I wouldn't let him dig a new hole for my outhouse."

Nub took another quick look back at the pair.

"You're aware of the rescue Alfonso and I executed on the cliff. What no one has related is that Bo wouldn't even proffer his gratitude. Indeed, once he was safe, he ordered the two of us to remove ourselves from his path."

"I'd've throwed the SOB back off," snapped Jake.

"I assume he was embarrassed to have someone such as us save his life."

"Some people don't need no reason to be a bastard."

"For all your disapproval of me, sir, at least you respect Dru enough not to level an epithet on me. Two times, Bo has called me a 'dirty Siwash.' "

Jake's face darkened, and he looked over his shoulder with narrowed eyes.

"I'd knock him on his butt if he was to call you that in front of me," he growled. "I'd damned sure do it."

Nub let the remark linger as their horses wended through the shadow of a hoodoo. Dru's father seemed to be a man of unshakable convictions, but Nub began to see in him a complex individual. Opinionated, intolerant, and intransigent — just a day ago, they would all have been words by which to describe him. But Jake's repeated defense of Nub marked him as someone who may not have fully believed what he outwardly projected.

"That's twice now you've supported me by your words, Mr. Graves," Nub said as they broke into bright sunshine again. "For that too, I'm appreciative."

Jake glared at him. "Listen," he snarled, "I ain't forgot for a minute what you done at headquarters." He ground his jaw. "I could've stopped all this, spared them girls a hell you and me can't even imagine. It would've been over and done with if wasn't for you."

"Sir, we virtually match their force in size now. Don't you think —"

"Hell, both Cappses put together couldn't hurt Dru and Ruthie the way you done. Maybe I don't call you a dirty Siwash, but that don't mean you ain't one."

Gigging his Appaloosa, the older man surged ahead, leaving the dark shadow of another hoodoo falling over Nub.

Sun or no sun, Nub's world stayed dark as he rode alone, reappraising his actions at headquarters in light of the outrage to which Jake had alluded. As terrible as the image of Dru's grave had been, it paled before the brutality he pictured now, and he welcomed the moment when Alfonso pulled abreast on his chestnut.

"You quiet, *Señor* Nub."

"Troubled and disheartened, I suppose."

"Dis-?"

"Lo siento," apologized Nub, realizing he needed to simplify. "Down in the dumps, we say. *Sabe?*"

"*Sí*, when my family all *muerta*, dead, everything go black like night even with sun in sky."

Nub studied him, a slight *muchacho* with an ear caked with dried blood and an arm that he held close to tender ribs. The sixteen-year-old had lost his entire world and somehow had managed to carry on, and even now he chased after the very bandits who had assaulted him at headquarters.

"I cannot emphasize enough how much I admire you, Alfonso," said Nub. "You've faced so much adversity — bad things — and yet here you are, riding alongside us."

"*Mi papá*, he always tell me it not enough for a *hombre* to know how to ride. He must know how to fall."

Nub had never before taken time to speak at length with Alfonso, and he regretted now that he hadn't. This was a *muchacho* of more depth than he had realized.

"You obviously learned well from him,

and at a young age," said Nub. "You were already in the Cross C's employ when I arrived."

"*Sí,* I come up from *río* when twelve, after *mi papá* die. But I on my own much time after Mama die and Papa go off hunting *tlahuelpuchi.*"

"Hunting *tlahuelpuchi*?"

"*Sí,* he spend much time up and down *río,* both sides. When my *hermana,* baby sister, die *chupado por el brujo* — sucked by the witch — Mama die too, even though she still alive. '*Mi niña,* my baby!' she cried, and it go on for four years, '*Mi niña, mi niña!'* She never say other words. Then she go sleep one night and never wake up.

"Papa know about Rentería the *tlahuelpuchi* from Rentería's brother, and when Mama die, he leave me and go hunt for *tlahuelpuchi.* Papa grow up in Tlaxcala — *sabe* Tlaxcala? — and know how to kill *tlahuelpuchi.* When he hear babies die *chupado por el brujo,* he go there, ask questions, village after village. But people scared when Papa ask so much, and some think Papa himself might be *tlahuelpuchi.* They hang *mi papá* and I come to Cross C's."

"My Lord!" exclaimed Nub.

For troubling seconds, Alfonso could say

no more, for his chin quivered and his cheeks began to glisten. Then the boy wiped his nose with his sleeve and firmed up his jaw.

"Now I hunt Rentería the *tlahuelpuchi* like *mi papá*. He kill my sister, and he same as kill Mama and Papa too."

Nub couldn't imagine being sixteen and carrying that kind of burden.

"*Señorita* Ruthie good to me," Alfonso continued. "She teach me to speak the English. The other *señorita* too. We get them back, I kill *tlahuelpuchi* way *mi papá* show me."

"There's a particular way of dispatching? By that, I mean killing?"

"Oh, *sí, Señor* Nub. Two ways kill *tlahuel-puchi* or he come back, *muy poderóso,* stronger than before. *Tlahuelpuchi* either kill himself, or . . ."

Dangling by cord from Alfonso's saddle horn was a worn, leather scabbard, and from it the *muchacho* drew a machete with hammer marks showing in its hand-forged blade. The weapon was stained and rusted in places, but as he twisted it in the sunlight, the blade glinted where it mattered most: in the eighteen-inch edge that seemed finely honed.

"The *padre* bless it," explained the boy.

"He dip it in blood that flow from statue of Our Lady. Way I kill *tlahuelpuchi* is —"

With the machete, Alfonso simulated two swift chops in the air.

"No head," he added, "Rentería the *tlahuelpuchi* die."

As would Rentería the man, thought Nub.

Just one more chance.

That's all Jake wanted, one last chance to listen to wisdom rather than heart, to take action, no matter how reprehensible, based on necessity rather than emotion.

At sixteen, it had been too much to ask of him. Down the sights of his Sharp's carbine, he had watched a Comanche devil sweep his sister up across a paint horse and carry her away through the big, twisted live oaks so they could violate her. Young Jake had joined with neighboring homesteaders and tracked the band clear to the San Saba River, only to find her facedown beside a dormant honeysuckle shrub, the shadow tracks of circling buzzards playing on her naked back. To this day, the sweet smell of a honeysuckle's white blooms still soured Jake's stomach.

All those years ago, he had failed his sister, failed himself, failed all that was good in the world. And just yesterday at headquarters, through no fault of his own, he had failed his daughter and niece.

Just one more chance to see them down his sights . . .

If there was no other choice, that's all he wanted. But he couldn't forget what Nub had tried to tell him, that they no longer chased after thirty-five or forty bandits, but six. Hell, what kind of man would sulk over not being allowed to kill his own daughter and niece, just because an Indian might have been right in preventing him?

Lost in turmoil, Jake fell off the pace and rode head-down until his Appaloosa stopped. Looking up, he found himself bunched with the other riders in a dry arroyo lined with allthorn and javelina bush. To his left, the tracks of horses and wild burros marked the way east up the drainage.

Jake's Appaloosa began pawing at the gravelly bed, and Alfonso's chestnut and the blazed-face roan did the same. Digging for water was a horse's instinctive response to thirst, and Jake understood why the bandits had veered with the burros' course. The tough, dry trek from the Cross C's was taking a toll on the horses of allies and enemies alike, and finding a water hole was all but essential.

Jake quickly fell into self-reflection again, and he rode that way up the arroyo until he met a strong headwind and drew rein at the mouth of a narrow canyon with wagon-sized boulders. The other searchers were already there, and on both sides the towering walls rose in tiers, vertical gray rock punctuated by green-tinged levels with sotol, barrel cacti, prickly pear, and lechuguilla.

Twisting in the saddle, Jake scanned the bandits' trail. The horse tracks clearly entered the canyon, but doubled back and struck out south again along the range's base.

Meanwhile, his Appaloosa had begun pawing once more.

"Damp here," he noted, checking under his horse's breast. "I expect they's water enough for the horses up-canyon a ways."

Then Nub's voice drew Jake's attention.

"I do not like the implications of this."

The foreman was off his horse and speaking as he ran his fingers along a standing slab of limestone on the right, and Jake shifted his Appaloosa so he could see between Alfonso and the Cappses. In the face of the rock was a fresh etching, and as Nub's forefinger traced it, Jake made out the figure of a star inside a circle. Two of the five points were directed upward, and

154

inside the star was a crude sketch of a horned thing that might have been a goat.

"*¡Madre de Dios!*" exclaimed Alfonso. "The *diablo* card!"

"What the hell's the wetback jabberin'?" asked Bill Ike.

"It's the Sabbatic Goat," explained Nub, "popularized by de Guaita twenty years ago, with antecedents dating back much farther."

"So what's it mean?" asked Bo.

"A symbol of the occult. A tarot deck has a similar representation known as the devil card."

"*Tlahuelpuchi* do this!" said Alfonso. "He call up *diablo*!"

"*Call* him up?" Bill Ike leaned to the side so he could rub the bottom of his thigh. "Way ever'thing sticks, stings, or bites out here, how far away can ol' Fork-ed Tail ever get?"

"I would temper any belittling remarks concerning the devil, Mr. Capps," said Nub. "Even the archangel Michael didn't dare censure him, but asked the Almighty to do it."

"*Diablo muy poderóso,* very strong," said Alfonso, nervously glancing about.

"I sure don't want nothing to do with the SOB," opined Bo.

"Boy, find some backbone," chided his

father. "Take a nip if you got to. The devil's just a ol' wives' tale."

Abruptly, from somewhere up-canyon came a long, low moan, and Jake wasn't alone in turning quickly and searching the jumbled boulders.

"Good God, what is that?" asked Bo.

"*¡Dios mío!*" exclaimed Alfonso.

The moan died away as suddenly as it had come, but even Jake felt a chill.

Bill Ike laughed nervously. "I-god, ain't that wind somethin'. Make a man go to imaginin' all sorts of things, if he was to let it."

For once, Jake agreed with Bill Ike. The only way a made-up thing like the devil could hurt a man was if he dwelled on it to the point that he lost focus on the dangers around him. And in a place like this, with armed killers ahead and an uncaring desert pressing in on all sides, a man's safety demanded every moment of his attention.

Even if Jake's was divided too many ways.

Nub mounted up and led the way on into the canyon, where the two-way tracks weaved through dwarfing boulders that hid anything more than yards away. The bottom was largely gravel, but whenever hoofs crossed table rock, the drum played between the tiered walls.

156

As Jake squeezed his Appaloosa through the maze, he found himself close on the hindquarters of Bill Ike's stocking-footed bay.

"All we's done is sure wearin' on a man," said Bill Ike. He checked over his shoulder. "What's all this worth to you, Graves?"

Jake just looked at him.

"I figure Ruthie's folks ain't gonna be happy about my boy marryin' her," Bill Ike added.

You figure right, thought Jake, staying quiet.

"Imagine they'll need persuadin'."

Persuadin', and then some.

Bill Ike ducked under a hanging screwbean limb, the thorns rasping across his hat. "You's her uncle. By marriage, anyhow. Once we get her back, it'd sure help if you was to put in a good word for Bo. You know, how he took it on hisself to go after her. Took a lot of gumption, what he done."

Jake held his stare.

"He near died on that cliff," reminded Bill Ike. "Figure that counts for somethin'."

Jake wanted to tell Bill Ike to go to hell, and to take that drunk of a son with him. But he held his tongue, knowing he had to keep his small force together.

"So what's it worth, gettin' your daughter

and niece back?" pressed Bill Ike with another look back.

Jake struggled to give a measured response that would keep the Cappses committed. "I'd trade my life straight up for them two," he said quietly.

"My boy'd sure be good for that girl. Makes sense for the Cross C's too, joinin' the two outfits. Just the tonic for hard times."

Then Bill Ike added something that tested Jake's resolve to hold his tongue.

"I'm a-countin' on you, Graves. Me and my boy both."

As they maneuvered up-canyon, the wind howled between boulders and set the limbs of desert willows screeching. Jake could smell the dampness now, a briny taste that hung in his throat, and between the rhythmic hoofbeats, he began to distinguish a patter like big drops of falling rain.

Strangely, the closer he came to the source, the more uneasy he became. All the way from the Cross C's, he had feared that he would find Dru and Ruthie lying face-down like his sister. That prospect was no less real now, but this trepidation was something more, something that made him search left and right for a presence he knew he wouldn't see. Annie had spoken to him of fallen angels and demons, but this was the first time he had found a reason to question whether the idea was just nonsense.

For a proud, stubborn man like Jake, it was a humbling moment.

Then, beyond another willow, he rounded a final boulder and burst upon the head of a box canyon. Twenty yards away, past shin-high maidenhair ferns in scattered rocks, an intimidating pour-off rose up, its water-worn face glinting with a dozen thin streams falling individually. Side by side, they splashed into a small pool surrounded by cattails, as wet a place as Jake had seen in this country. Even away from the falls, water seeped from every crack in the cliff and dripped from clinging patches of green moss.

But if this was such a peaceful oasis, why did Jake feel the way he did? Even his Appaloosa was skittish, and as he tried to bring the horse under control, he noticed that everyone's mount was similarly spooked. Water should have been the horses' foremost concern, but instead they focused on something to the left, for the ears of every animal pointed in that direction.

A big, gnarly mesquite blocked Jake's view, and he took his Appaloosa out a few feet more and saw the dark opening of a cave fifteen feet above the canyon bottom. A rocky slope led up to it from left to right, and the shining lid of an opened can on the ledge at top told Jake that at least one of the Mexicans had ascended only a short time before. The jagged entrance was about four feet high and almost as wide, and the degree of darkness inside suggested a deep recess.

"Got the horses shook up," said Jake, nodding to the cave. "Lion must be denned up in there."

"No, *señor,*" said Alfonso. "It *la cueva del diablo,* devil cave!"

Bill Ike drew his revolver. "I-god, I hate them panthers," he said, obviously disregarding the *muchacho.* "Regular calf killers."

But Bo didn't shrug off Alfonso's remark so easily. "What's that mean, devil cave? You been here before?"

"Oh, no, this first time," said Alfonso. "But cave like a door to *infierno,* hell. *Tlahuelpuchi,* he go in every cave. He meet with *el diablo.*"

"Wet's at it again," said Bill Ike with a derisive laugh.

"Let's hear him out, Bill Ike!" urged Bo.

The *muchacho* pointed to the entrance. "Is why I say *la cueva del diablo,* devil cave.

Diablo make *tlahuelpuchi más fuerte,* much stronger."

"Aw, hell, let's get the horses to the water hole," said Bill Ike.

Watering the animals was a priority, all right, but as Jake dismounted and handed his reins to Alfonso, the cave dominated his thoughts. If the Mexicans had gone inside, they might have dragged Dru and Ruthie with them, and he wouldn't ride out of here until he assured himself that the girls weren't lying up there dead.

Sliding his Marlin carbine out of its saddle scabbard, he started for the cave with a shudder. Gaining the steep slope, he crept up it in fear, hoping to meet a mountain lion or the devil himself rather than find again what he had under that honeysuckle bush. Halfway up, his boots slipped and he dropped to his knees, just as he had sunk at his mother's feet when he had returned home from the fresh grave on the San Saba. Even now, across time and distance, he heard her grief-stricken words as clearly as if they echoed through the canyon.

"It ain't your fault, Jake. Jake, it ain't your fault."

He could still feel her comforting hands on the back of his head, still feel his eyes sting as she had drawn him under her breast.

"Let the Lord take your hurt away," she had sobbed. "My poor darlin', just let Him lift you up . . . lift you up . . ."

Suddenly Jake was on his feet and stooped at the cave entrance, and from the dense shadows inside broke the same weird moan as before.

"My Lord!"

Jake didn't know which alarmed him most, the mournful cry from the *diablo* cave or Nub's sudden exclamation from behind. Checking, Jake found the foreman almost at his shoulder, the pump action shotgun poised to deliver a load of buckshot.

"Easy!" warned Jake. "Watch where you's pointin' that thing!"

Jake would never have admitted it, but he was glad to have Nub at his back. Staring inside the cave again, he felt an outward-blowing wind. In moments, the current lessened and the moaning died away, replaced by a low soughing that still gave Jake reason to keep a firm grip on his carbine.

"Not like any lion *I* ever heard," he tried to assure himself.

Indeed, he smelled the dank, stagnant odor of a cave rather than the strong musk of a panther. Nevertheless, past the first few feet everything inside was lost in the gloom, and Jake had no choice but to brush through the entrance and strike a match from his pocket.

His eyes weren't adjusted to the shadows, so the flare didn't show much, just a room-sized chamber barely high enough for him to stand. But when the persistent breeze extinguished the match, Jake saw a small pile of live coals at ten o'clock. The carbine was ready at his hip, and he took the precaution of scanning the cave for glowing eyes before he went to the embers.

The coals seemed to have a pulse, changing from red to yellow to red, and he could taste the bitter smoke as it rose. He struck another match, this time cupping the flame with his hand, and confirmed with relief that the cave was otherwise empty. Meanwhile, the wind continued its forlorn lament through pitch-black holes that only a rattler could have navigated.

"At your feet, Mr. Graves."

Until Nub's alert, Jake didn't realize that the foreman had accompanied him inside, but now a scrap of paper between Jake's boot and the coals had the attention of both men. The match went out as Jake picked it up, and he carried the scrap with him as he followed Nub outside to the ledge.

Jake was surprised to find Alfonso there, brandishing a machete.

"No *tlahuelpuchi?*" asked the *muchacho,* peering around Jake's shoulder.

"No devil, neither," said Jake. "Fire in there, though. Piece of paper with scribblin' on it."

Jake held the paper out at arm's length, trying to read it with aging eyes.

"What does it say, Mr. Graves?" asked Nub.

"Mex, ain't it? I speak it better than I read it."

He passed the scrap to Nub, who translated as he read.

Oh, Diablo! Let me into the deepest part of your being. I know that you're here. I can feel you. I've come to your holy place to beg your favor. I ask that the blood of the men who follow us be spilled for your pleasure. So it is, and so it will be!

"Santa Maria, a death spell!" exclaimed Alfonso.

Jake didn't know what to think, and a quick look at Nub's face told him that he wasn't alone. Together they turned to *la cueva del diablo,* and its shadows now seemed to grasp for him like a living thing.

164

As a chilling moan broke again from the depths, Jake shrank with an oath.

"Let's water them horses and get the hell out of here."

CHAPTER 9

Standing with the other men beside the watering horses, Jake felt it first under his boots, a quick jolt that rushed up through his legs.

His Appaloosa noticed it too, for the bronc jerked its head up. All at once, five horses were ready to bolt, prompting Jake to lunge and seize the Appaloosa's bridle. Still, the horse was almost unmanageable, for the ground was shaking and the canyon walls rumbled, spilling dirt and rocks from the heights and disrupting the pour-off's flow.

"What the hell!" exclaimed Bill Ike.

"Temblor!" yelled Nub.

The ground began to roll underfoot, a violent sway that staggered Jake and set the Appaloosa squealing. To a roar, bluffs collapsed on either side, the landslides generating powerful winds thick with dust. Striking from multiple directions, they blinded and choked, and for a moment all Jake could do was cling to the bridle as the Appaloosa slung its head. Then he felt his way along the animal's neck to the saddle horn and stirrup and swung astride.

Jake had lost all sense of direction, but he gave the horse its head and let the bronc's night vision and instinct take over. The horse leaped forward and they were away in the wildest ride of Jake's life, a desperate flight across tossing ground.

Hard rock scraped his leg and he dodged punishing limbs as the Appaloosa careened through boulders. Debris rained down on his hat and shoulders and he expected to be crushed at any instant, but he held on even when the horse pulled up sharply and threw him against its neck. A brute shape was ahead, blocking the Appaloosa's way, and from it came a faint cry.

Jake leaned over and extended his arm, a precarious position even before someone clutched it and pulled him out of the stirrups. The next thing Jake knew, he was down, a helpless figure stomped by the hard heels of a pair of boots. A hoof glanced off Jake's brow and the horse was away again, and it took only a moment of writhing to realize that someone else was in the saddle and leaving him to die.

Jake was so damned mad that he could

have chewed nails, but rage wouldn't get him out of this alive. Gaining his feet and struggling to breathe, he felt his way from one rocking boulder to the next, a man lost in time and place. But he had already been lost for almost half a century, with nothing but his mother's words to carry him. Now they came again, strangely soothing despite the shaking earth and falling bluffs and all the burdens that he carried.

"Let Him lift you up . . . lift you up . . . lift you up . . ."

Abruptly it was over, the quaking and the thunder and the landslides, but dust still hung in the air like a thick fog when Jake stumbled out of the canyon. The others were already there, holding all five horses, and only now did he consider which of them had abandoned him in such a grim moment.

There was surly Bill Ike, flapping his hat against his trouser leg to shake off the dust, and Bo, not unexpectedly swigging from a bottle. Alfonso was nearby, down on a knee as he lifted the chestnut's foreleg in inspection, and Nub was beyond, his back turned as he checked a bloody spot on the face of the Appaloosa.

Jake's Appaloosa.

It was strong evidence, even if circumstances didn't virtually rule out everyone else.

Bill Ike was a sorry bastard, and his son equally worthless, but they depended on Jake to curry the favor of Ruthie's parents. Alfonso was just a boy, and prone to an adolescent's whims, but Jake couldn't think of any reason the *muchacho* would want him out of the picture. Nub, though . . .

Of all of them, wasn't he the only one who had anything to gain by it? If Dru could be rescued, wouldn't it be a simple matter to convince only Annie to accept their marriage? Hell, she did already.

No matter who had left Jake in the canyon, maybe panic instead of malice was to blame. But Jake was tired and hurting and he wanted to take it out on somebody. With a snort, he started for Nub.

The foreman must have heard him brushing through the creosote bushes, for he turned.

"Mr. Graves! You're out safely," he said.

"Yeah."

"With the dust dissipating, I was preparing to prosecute a search."

"That so?"

Stopping at the Appaloosa's hindquarter, Jake ran his hand along the bronc's coat and stirred up dust. "You ride my horse out of there?"

"Sir?"

Setting his jaw firmly, Jake faced him and pictured Dru in this damned Indian's arms. "I think you know what I'm a-askin'."

"No, I succeeded in reaching my sorrel." Nub nodded to the thick-maned animal tied to a nearby scrub mesquite. "It's obvious now why the horses were so anxious upon reaching the pour-off. They doubtless sensed the impending quake."

Nub had changed the subject, and Jake didn't care to listen. Turning, he scanned the *muchacho* and the Cappses.

"Who was it come out on the Appaloosa?" he shouted.

Bill Ike and Bo didn't look up, but from the other side of the chestnut, Alfonso stood and looked across at Jake.

"See *nada*, nothing, *Señor* Jake."

"Mr. Graves, am I to construe that you were purposely left without a mount?" spoke up Nub.

Jake faced him again. "Pulled off of my horse is more like it. Damned near died while one of you was savin' his own neck."

"Sir, I assure you that it wasn't I. Whether the Appaloosa came out with a rider, or on its own, I'm unable to say. All I knew was that you were not among us, and it con-

170

cerned me. I was anxious for the dust to disperse so I could go in search."

Nub sounded sincere, and maybe Jake had jumped to the wrong conclusion anyway. He took another look at Alfonso and the Cappses and considered the upheaval that all of them had faced in the canyon. In that kind of fix, could he really blame anyone for acting in his own self-interest? Regardless, wouldn't the girls be better served if he just shut up and kept this shaky alliance intact?

The small campfire against the arroyo's low bank made the night beyond seem not only darker, but strangely threatening.

Jake had chosen this spot carefully, for it was far enough from a hoodoo to be safe in an aftershock, and deep enough for the bank to hide the fire from the Mexicans. But as he sat around it with the others, the night seemed to reach out for him like the gloom of *la cueva del diablo.*

Damn it, why was he allowing foolish notions to play on his mind? Why not just finish his beans and crawl in his bedroll?

But the wild talk over the crackle of the fire wouldn't let him.

"Show them, *señor,*" Alfonso was saying. The shadow of his arm danced against the bank as he motioned to Nub. "Show what *tlahuelpuchi* leave in cave for *el diablo*. It death spell!"

"Death spell? What's that?" Bo asked. His slurred speech was almost unintelligible, but his anxiety was clear.

"Sharing it would prove counterproductive," Nub told the *muchacho*.

"What's a death spell?" Bo asked again. He had drunk heavily since the earthquake, and the firelight reflected in his bottle as he took another nip and faced Nub. "You got something, show it, you . . ."

Bo wisely let his voice trail away, but Jake agreed with Nub that the note itself might inflame tensions.

"You didn't save that scratchin', did you?" he asked the foreman. "Here, let me see it."

Nub produced the note from his pocket and passed it to him. Jake wanted only to discard it, but he was momentarily drawn to the words as the firelight flickered on the page.

"Ain't anybody going to tell me?" pressed Bo. "What's this death spell?"

"My boy's havin' a conniption, Graves," said Bill Ike. "Read it to him."

Jake knew better. Crumpling the page, he tossed it in the fire.

"I-god, Graves," snapped Bill Ike. He took

172

up a stick and raked the wadded paper out of the flames. "My boy won't sleep a wink 'less he reads that thing."

When Bill Ike took up the page and looked it over, Jake saw that it had curled and scorched. Nevertheless, the pencil script must have remained legible.

"All writ in Meskin, callin' on the devil," said Bill Ike, squinting his eyes. "Wantin' him to spill our blood so's we'll quit a-followin'."

Bo gave an oath and took a long, hard drink, but his father only laughed.

"What them dumb Mexes can come up with," he snorted.

"Look what happened, Bill Ike!" argued Bo, the fire wild in his eyes. "The whole canyon come down on us! Don't be telling me that was all just chance!"

Jake wondered. "Had a quake in these parts last spring," he reminded Bo.

"Indeed," agreed Nub. "It caused considerable damage at headquarters."

There was a note in the foreman's voice that made Jake question whether Nub was any surer of a coincidence than he was.

"Mr. Capps," Nub added, "you must have experienced the spring quake on your place as well."

"Nope," said Bill Ike. "On a train in

Kansas with my yearlings, Bo and me both. Saw where things been shook up when we got back."

"That was better than eight months ago!" contended Bo. "I don't like none of this, Bill Ike!"

He jumped up, too quickly for someone so drunk, and when he spun to search the dark, he went off-balance and was unable get his feet under him. For a moment he stumbled around like a cow with the blind staggers, and then he mumbled something and fell flush across the fire.

Wood popped and embers flew, and only quick anticipation kept Jake from catching a flaming stick in the eye. He would just as soon have let the damned fool roast, but Bo's wallowing stirred sparks that rose into the night, a dead giveaway to their position. With the combined efforts of Jake on one side and Bill Ike and Nub on the other, they dragged Bo from the fire, his bootheels raking coals out with him.

"Boy, you all right?" asked Bill Ike, slapping out smoldering places on his son's clothes. "Tell me somethin', boy."

But his son couldn't answer, and Jake realized why. Bo was passed out stone-cold drunk.

"Hell," said Bill Ike, standing. "I'll just lay his beddin' over him. Come mornin', I'm chewin' his butt out."

For once, Bill Ike was true to his word. Jake had no sooner begun stirring in his bedroll at daybreak than he heard at a distance a gruff voice berating Bo.

"Get over here, boy. Got somethin' to thrash out."

"I'm hurting, Bill Ike," whined Bo.

"You oughta be, passin' out in the fire that away."

"Got burned places on my arm. Legs too."

"Been worse if we hadn't drug you out. What do you think Graves thinks about it?"

"Who cares what he thinks?" Bo moaned. "Told you, I'm hurting."

Jake snugged his blankets around his shoulders and rolled over so that he could see their shadowy outlines thirty yards down the arroyo.

"Hell of a impression you makin' on him," continued Bill Ike. "How you expect to get in good at the Cross C's 'less Graves was to speak up for you? Some story *he'll* have to tell: Yeah, that Capps boy got drunker than a fiddler's bitch and passed out in the fire."

"Make me a prickly pear poultice, will you, Bill Ike?"

"You got to quit this drinkin' all time," the older man went on. "Nobody can stand bein' around you."

"Yeah? What else a soul to do when he has to put up with you?" For the first time, Jake heard energy in Bo's voice. "I've a good mind to tell Graves who I saw ride out on his Appaloosa."

"You smartin' off to me, boy?" Bill Ike demanded.

"I'm a grown man. I'll say what I want. I'm not the little boy you used to beat out of plain meanness every day. Started drinking young to ease the hurting. And I don't mean just from the bruises, either."

"Didn't know I was raisin' a drunk. Always tried to bring you up right."

"Like hell, you old bastard," said Bo. "I never was good enough for you. That's why you lit into me so much. Hadn't been good enough ever since you found out I wasn't yours."

Bill Ike went quiet for a moment, and when he spoke again, his voice was subdued.

"Told you never to speak about that no more. I raised you. Makes you the same as flesh and blood."

For long seconds, there was silence — a painful silence for the two of them, Jake imagined — and when he heard Bill Ike's voice again, there was a tenderness in it he had never heard before.

"Come here, boy. Sorry you's a-hurtin' so. Let's get a poultice fixed up for them burns."

CHAPTER 10

Rentería had come back.

Set flush against a creosote-covered hill close to the Rio Grande, the sun-baked *jacal* of Elena Sabana spoke to him from across the decades. It was a simple, north-facing hut constructed on a framework of poles standing side by side and daubed with mud and grass. On its dirt-packed roof, the ribs of the underlying ocotillo thatching showed in the long morning shadows. Crudely rocked in front, the dwelling was deeper than it was wide, with a hovering boulder serving as the rear wall.

The *señora* had been among the first to immigrate to the border from Tlaxcala, and she had brought with her not only a *curandera's* healing knowledge, but a *tezlitac's* control over the weather. From his family roots in central Mexico, Rentería knew the Aztec word *tezlitac* as "one who throws hail," but Sabana also had the power to ward off evil.

Or so Rentería had hoped after his first kill.

At sixteen, with the taste of his sister's blood fresh on his lips, Rentería had come here in search of help. The *tezlitac* had seemed old even then, a wizened woman with a face like cracked saddle leather. But the memory of her hands was the most vivid. Her fingers had been gnarled with age, and when she had taken both of his hands in hers across a small table, he had felt a fire up through his arms.

Her dark eyes had gone wide in fear, and she had recoiled from his touch.

"*Fuera de aquí* — get out!" she had cried. "Take your evil with you!"

How she had sensed his alliance with *el diablo,* Rentería still didn't know. But he had fled terrified, a *muchacho* adrift in a purgatory that continued today as he drew rein at the *jacal* with Consuela-who-wasn't-Consuela and her feverish *amiga.*

Now, as then, the *tezlitac* stood hunched over in the open doorway, her shriveled figure framed against the shadows inside. She seemed largely unchanged, as if she had just stepped across the decades to face him again. Her short straight hair, starkly white against the background, was parted down the middle, and tiny shells dangled from her ears. Most striking, her brow had vertical scoring as she pinched her eyes together in a penetrating stare that made Rentería uncomfortable.

Then Sabana redirected her gaze, and she must have seen the yellow-haired *señorita* bent over the saddle horn of the bay.

"She is sick?" asked Sabana.

"*Muy.* From lechuguilla," acknowledged Rentería.

Indeed, across the merciless desert and shaking ground of the previous day, the young woman had struggled to stay in the stirrups. The long night had been no better, for she had tossed and moaned as Consuela's devil twin had tended her. Today she slumped even more, necessitating that she be tied again to the horn for her own safety.

"I have *mucho dinero,*" added Rentería.

"A *curandera* takes no payment." Then the old woman cocked her head to the side. "Maybe so if you want Sabana the *tezlitac* to bring the hail, eh?"

Rentería glanced back at the way from which they had come. She had given him an idea.

"Bring her in," said the healer.

Rentería instructed his men to untie the ill *señorita,* and he allowed Consuela-who-wasn't-Consuela to stay with her as they carried her inside to a single gloomy room. The floor was of packed clay, and the ceiling hung so low that Rentería's sombrero brushed the thatching. Supporting the roof down the center were three standing cottonwood timbers, silhouetted against the glow of a small fire in back. The place was drafty, and he could smell the swirling woodsmoke as Sabana led them past the last leaning post.

Removing a few items from a crude table, the old woman directed Rentería's men to place the sick woman across it. The table creaked and wobbled, but once she was stretched out, Rentería emptied a pouch of coins on the tabletop, the jingling silver shining in the firelight.

He looked up and found Sabana's piercing gaze again.

"Bring the hail," he said.

Sabana motioned in question to the moaning woman whose beaded face was flushed with fever.

"First *el granizo,* the hail," said Rentería. "Back to the north, *por favor.*"

Nodding, Sabana shuffled to the deeper shadows on the left. Now in the role of *tezlitac,* she whispered an incantation as she rummaged, and when she went to the fire, she threw a pinch of powder that made the flames gasp and leap. Her eyes rolled up into their sockets as she repeated the process eight times, and before it was over, her own face was wet with sweat. When she returned to the table, she trembled as if the ritual had drained much of her energy.

"It's done?" asked Rentería.

Once more, she stared at him as if he stirred a troubling memory that eluded her. Rentería, more ill at ease, glanced out the doorway and saw no sign of storm clouds to the north.

"*Tezlitac?*" he asked again.

"Soon. Very soon."

Turning her attention to the feverish *señorita,* Sabana inspected her facial wounds and bloodstained clothes. All the while, Consuela's devil twin stroked her *amiga's* yellow tresses and soothed with quiet words. Upon assessing her condition, the *curandera* went to a nearby metate and set to grinding seeds with a mano.

"*¿Qué es?*" asked Rentería.

"*Toloache.* For the fever."

Rentería knew *toloache,* or nightshade, as leaves to be smoked to bring on visions, but he trusted the *curandera* to know its other uses. Upon reducing the seeds to a flour, Sabana added it to a pot of water and placed it on the coals to brew. Next, she ground dried sagebrush into masa and rubbed it into the facial wounds. Before treating the lacerations hidden by clothing, Sabana waved Rentería and his men outside.

When she allowed them to return, Consuela-who-wasn't-Consuela was lifting her *amiga's* shoulders so the *curandera* could trickle the *toloache* brew between her lips. After several gurgling swallows, Sabana poured the remainder into a dried gourd and sealed it with a wadded cloth.

"She may go," she said, extending it. "Take this for her."

Accepting the gourd, Rentería found Sabana's eyes in a hard stare again, as if she probed his very soul. Shaken, he wanted away from her, and he passed the brew to the devil twin and stayed close on the heels of his men as they carried the *señorita* outside. But just as he reached the doorway, something compelled him to stop and look back.

The *tezlitac* approached, one slow step at a time, and soon the two of them were face-to-face, suspended between daylight and shadow. Now more than ever, her eyes held him in their spell, and when she reached down for his hands, he didn't resist.

The moment he felt her touch, a charge

like an electrical shock seemed to race up through his shoulders, gripping him as powerfully as it had when he had been a *muchacho.*

"You!" she exclaimed. "The child of *el diablo*!"

Never had Rentería felt so vulnerable, so in need, and from deep inside came a decades-old urgency to escape his curse.

"There's no help for me?" he asked. "What do I have to do, *tezlitac*?"

"Die!" she whispered. "By your own hand — die, *tlahuelpuchi*!"

Just as he had so many years before, Rentería turned and ran, a man possessed or demented but no less lost either way.

Nub's horse was uneasy, and the morning sky told him why.

As he and the others rode south, tracing the hoofprints through a flat with creosote and cacti, ominous clouds gathered in the west. To a growing rumble, the sorrel threw up its nose and snorted. A few strides farther, just past an isolated Spanish dagger, the horse reared a little and pawed the air. Later, as it broke and ran, Nub anticipated and managed to weather half a dozen jumps. Even when he drew rein sharply, the slowing sorrel cold-jawed and tried to go in a circle.

As Nub brought the horse under control, he found himself alongside Bo and his blazed-face roan on drag.

"If our eyes didn't adequately convey matters, our mounts have made things apparent," said Nub.

"Do *what*?"

"A storm is developing," simplified Nub. "The horses give warning."

"Think I hadn't figured that out?" Bo moaned.

Bo was as unfriendly as ever, but maybe he had added reason. Grimacing in pain, he rode slumped with an arm across his chest. Notably, from the time they had broken camp, he had stayed a full fifty yards behind Bill Ike. It was the first time Nub had seen the two apart, and he supposed that a drunken moment in a fire explained why. Indeed, their heated exchange of early morning had carried distinctly up the arroyo, and despite Bill Ike's overtures, Bo had kept his distance ever since.

"A thunderstorm in December is becoming less of a meteorological oddity," Nub remarked. "Considering the strength of the one last week, we should make contingency plans."

Bo grunted. "Yeah," he said sarcastically, "we can head straight for the barn out here, can't we? Plan, hell."

"Seriously, Capps, you should not dismiss the notion out of hand."

Bo's face swelled. "There's a *mister* in front of my name. You damned sure better know your place."

Nub knew it all too well. No matter his upbringing or education or character, he rode through a world that might deny him a future with Dru even if they rescued her.

"This isn't an appropriate venue to discuss my position in society," he said. "The storm is approaching."

Indeed, as Nub turned and lifted his gaze, he was startled to find how quickly the sky was disappearing. Sandy wisps had already climbed overhead, preparing the way for a dark, boiling bearcat that was the most frightening weather spectacle he had ever seen. Wicked lightning shot down out of an odd, greenish glow near center, but even as he felt the ground shake through the sorrel's legs, Nub was more concerned by the pedestal formation that abruptly dropped from the cloud's base. Black and rotating, dwarfing yucca as it hovered, it was a monster, and it came straight at them across a desert without shelter.

Nub rode on beside Bo as the thing settled over them like a hanging shroud, turning day into dusk. For a minute or two, there was an odd, almost peaceful lull, and then lightning cracked not a hundred yards away and hail began to fall.

Pea-sized at first, it tapped a tempo on Nub's hat and hopped on the ground like a swarm of big white insects. Driven by a sudden wind, the hail unnerved his horse, and when larger hailstones began to thud down with the smaller, he knew he had to act.

"Find a place to secure your mount!" he yelled to Bo.

Already, Nub was scouting — the too-distant Spanish dagger that marked the trail behind, the ocotillo stalks that thrashed ahead, the nearby prickly pear that trembled to more thunder. With little choice, he chose a thick creosote bush off to his right, knowing that its many stems and flexibility gave it strength.

"Remove your saddle!" he shouted as he gigged his horse for it.

"Who the hell are you to order me around?" Bo replied. "I'll damned sure do what I want to!"

Nub let him, for his own survival was at stake as he dismounted at the bush. A few hard, white rocks bigger than a fist had begun pounding down, and a man wouldn't be able to endure it.

Nub took a beating as he lashed the reins around the shrub's base, but it was nothing compared to the punishment he suffered in trying to unsaddle the shying horse. Never were cinch buckles so stubborn, but he finally dragged the saddle free.

Thirty-five pounds was a load in a fierce wind, but he crouched with the kack across his shoulder blades and felt blow after blow through the stout leather. He grimly held on, watching through the dangling tie straps as the hail rained down furiously, turning the ground white. A barreling train couldn't have been louder, and yet he could still hear the sorrel's pitiful moan.

Nub felt sorry for the animal, which could only turn its rump to the wind and bury its head between its knees. He had left the saddle blanket across the withers for protection, but hail the size of fists could knock a horse senseless.

Or crush a man's skull.

Bo!

Nub whirled in search. The storm was as blinding as it was relentless, allowing a clear view of only dragon's blood and other nearby shrubs that sagged under the barrage. If a man was more than a few yards away, Nub wouldn't have seen him, but beside a mangled agave at the limits of visibility, he made out a red blur. Stark against white, the stain was out of place, and even as Nub recognized it for what it was, he was up and rushing for it with the saddle over his shoulders.

Suddenly Bo was before him, down on hands and knees in the ice. Blood streamed down his face, the droplets flying as he shook his head like a dazed ram. Nub fell across him, shielding the injured man with his body as the saddle in turn shielded Nub. Bo must have been addled, for he tried to fight Nub off at first, and his confusion persisted as the hail continued to fall.

"It slipped out!" Bo mumbled. "I won't call you Papa! Don't whip me anymore, Bill Ike! It slipped out! I won't call you Papa!"

Bo went on, evidently reliving a bad memory, and Nub couldn't forget what he had overheard about his boyhood. Moments ago, if not for acting on instinct, Nub might have left the dissipated fool to his fate. Now, though, he couldn't keep from feeling a little compassion. How different might his own life have been if he hadn't been raised by such a caring man as Sam DeJarnett?

Bo quickly passed from one memory to another, and this one struck Nub in a special way, considering his relationship with the Cross C owners.

"Tell it again, Ruthie," whispered Bo. "You loving me, tell it again. Ruthie . . . Ruthie . . . You're the only thing good I got."

It had never occurred to Nub that maybe Ruthie really cared for Bo and that theirs was a real relationship, no matter his vices. Nub would never have believed it before, but now he wondered if Ruthie had found in this flawed individual something that he had overlooked.

Suddenly it was over, the wind and the hail and the crash of thunder, but a wasteland was all around as Nub removed the saddle. The storm had stripped the tiny-leafed creosotes bare and flattened the agave, lechuguilla, and bear grass. In one way, there was heavenly beauty in the ice that lay like a new snow, but the air had an odor like the sulfur he imagined burning in hell.

Bo seemed to be regaining his wits, and Nub let him struggle up on his own. There was a nasty cut on his forehead, and contusions elsewhere on his face, and he wobbled a little as he searched and found his beaten hat. Bo's roan was gone, but the sorrel still stood tied, no longer moaning, though appearing more ridden-down than ever.

Ahead, meanwhile, the older men and the *muchacho* stirred among their own horses.

Scanning the desert, Nub sighted the roan off to the west three hundred yards, and as soon as he saddled his horse and mounted up, he took the sorrel up alongside Bo and yielded the left stirrup.

"Step up."

There was reluctance in Bo's battered face, but he swung astride behind Nub and they were away to the west, the sorrel's hoofs crunching the unstable ice.

"Capps. *Mister* Capps." Nub tried out the courtesy title, the sound of it grating on him.

" 'Bout time you showed me respect, Indian."

If Bo wanted deference, he was his own worst enemy, but Nub continued.

"In your confused state, you said some things."

"Yeah, what?"

"That day I happened upon you and Miss Ruthie, I —"

"Should've knocked your teeth in, is what I should've done."

Nub was ready to go silent, but he cared enough about Ruthie to disregard the blather. "I assumed at the time your intentions were dishonorable."

"You damned —"

Maybe Bo didn't want to chase after his horse on foot, for he left off the epithet.

"Permit me to speak, please," said Nub.

"I'm a damned sight more honorable than you are. Indian, Mex, take your pick — you won't ever be a white man."

Nub ignored him. "Before you regained your faculties, you suggested that Miss Ruthie and you share legitimate affection."

"What the hell business is it of yours? You're nothing but hired help. First thing I'm doing after Ruthie and me's married is getting your butt fired."

"My concern is only for Miss Ruthie. If I wrongly intruded on a deeply personal moment that day last summer, I need to make amends to her once she's safe."

"Hadn't heard any apology for *me* out of you yet."

Bo seemed intent on making this as difficult as possible. For a while, there was only the crackle of ice under the hoofs as Nub formulated his words.

"Then confirm that she's expressed love for you."

"If you think you got to know, yeah, plenty of times. I'll take that apology now."

If the boor really expected an apology, he wasn't getting one. On the contrary, Nub pressed the issue.

"So the relationship is serious?"

"Enough of your prying, you damned Siwash. 'Fore long, you'll be gone from the Cross C's and me and the baby will be in. I —"

Bo must have realized what he had said, for he gave a quick gasp as Nub drew rein hard and turned to him.

"What baby?" asked Nub.

Despite the bruises, Bo was ashen, his jaw trembling and the white showing markedly in his eyes.

This was no time for respect. "Capps," Nub demanded, "what baby?"

Still, Bo only looked at him, beads of sweat popping out on his forehead.

"You royal bastard," said Nub.

Bo only sat there, a frightened man suspended against somber storm clouds that still churned as they receded.

"Her father will kill you," said Nub.

"He-He won't shoot a white man for it."

"If he doesn't, her uncle will. Jake Graves isn't a man to cross, and that extends to his niece as well."

"We get married quick enough, won't matter. Ruthie says if her folks won't have any of it, we'll run off and get it done. Time we come back, there'll be three of us and they'll take us in, no questions asked."

"Is Mr. Capps aware of all this?"

"Get me shot for sure, him bragging on it, he and his blood ties to the Cross C's." Then Bo's eyes seemed to plead. "You . . . You're not saying anything, are you? You won't be telling old man Graves, will you?"

With a sharp breath, Nub faced his pony's ears again. He had a horse to round up and bandits to overtake, and he couldn't let this troubling revelation rob him of focus.

CHAPTER 11

The strange blessing given to Ruthie stayed with Dru as their horses carried them downriver to the beat of eight sets of hoofs.

"Dos. Dios los bendiga."

Back at the *jacal,* with Rentería and his men waiting outside, the *curandera* had whispered the words upon taking Ruthie's wrist in her wrinkled hands.

"*Dos?* Two?" Dru had repeated. "What about two?"

"Her heart works for both."

Dru still hadn't understood, and the hunched little woman had turned.

"She is going to be a mother," the *curandera* had said.

A mother.

Now, three hours later, Dru looked at Ruthie riding abreast on her left, the blond hair tossing against inky storm clouds far away to the northeast. No longer secured to the saddle horn, Ruthie already sat her horse better, and the flush was gone from her face. Still, her nodding chin showed a person more asleep than awake, and maybe that was good. At least for a little while she might escape the nightmare they had lived since Christmas Day.

But what kind of added burden might Ruthie have been carrying silently?

The *curandera's* swift disclosure surely must have been wrong, but once Dru pieced things together, it wasn't so clear-cut. All week long before Christmas, Ruthie had stayed with her in Marfa, and twice before breakfast Ruthie had covered her mouth and run outside. "Somethin' I ate, I guess," she had explained. But there had also been her puzzling remarks about Bo Capps on the ride to the Cross C's, and Dru knew her cousin's mischief-making well enough to realize that she might have delighted in a forbidden relationship with a scalawag.

Now, as if stirred by Dru's thoughts, Ruthie lifted her head and turned. Her eyes were no longer glassy, but as she checked the riders ahead and behind, the soft cast of her face gave way to tension.

"They got us, Dru."

"You're awake — are you feeling better?"

Ruthie looked front and back again. "Oh, God, they still got us!"

Dru read the panic setting in once more. "Don't give up, Ruthie. They spotted somebody behind us yesterday. Nobody at home's going to rest till they get us back."

"What are we goin' to do? I-I don't remember — did these animals . . . Have they took . . . Oh, God!"

"They haven't touched us, Ruthie. You —"

"They must've, Dru! The way I —"

"Your horse fell with you, remember? Shin-daggers got you, and Rentería carried you to a *curandera.* You know, a Mexican healer."

Ruthie wrinkled her brow and brought fingers to her temple. "Dark . . . It was all dark, wasn't it? Made me drink somethin'." She gave look of disgust. "Oh, it was bitter!"

"It was medicine she fixed up. She treated the places you got stabbed and then had you drink something for the fever. I guess it worked, because you seem like you're better."

Ruthie calmed a little as they rode on, skirting streamside cottonwoods and black willows and throwing dust against woody grapevines that clung to a rock bluff away from the river.

"The *curandera* said something to me." Dru hesitated, wondering if this was the time. "You remember?"

Ruthie turned with a squint.

"Are . . . Are you sick at your stomach?" Dru added. "It's been happening a lot lately."

Ruthie answered with a long look.

"You know you can talk to me about anything, Ruthie," Dru reassured her.

Even with her eyes, Ruthie didn't acknowledge that she understood, but Dru couldn't help but notice that her cousin's fingers moved to her abdomen before she spoke.

"Not now, Dru, not here, not with *them.*" For a third time, Ruthie glanced over her shoulder. "If-If I could just be with Bo right now, the two of us, just together. God, Dru! I don't want them hurtin' my —"

"See, Consuela, I got help for your *amiga.*"

Dru didn't know that Rentería was near until he came up from behind, squeezing his black horse between Dru's dun and Ruthie's bay. Ruthie, clearly alarmed by his presence, immediately dropped back, leaving Dru to face a man so frightening and yet so seemingly insecure.

"Does it please you?" he asked. "I do good things, no? Tell me, Consuela."

Dru wanted to ask why he called her Consuela, but she was afraid it might break

198

whatever spell she apparently held on him. When she didn't respond whatsoever, Rentería appeared shaken.

"*Por favor,* what do you want from me?" he asked. "Why have you come back?"

"Just . . . Just let us go home," she appealed.

"*Sí,* to your *querencia,* where your heart still lives." Terrible anguish filled his leprous-like face. "My *querencia,* too, until the day went dark. *Lo siento,* I'm sorry! What I did, *lo siento!*"

Dru didn't think it possible to feel sympathy for someone so evil, but she almost did as his distraught voice continued to tremble.

"When . . . When you're there again, what will you do, Consuela? If I kneel and beg where the blood ran, will you go back to *infierno? Por favor,* go back and let me rest!"

Dru had never known anyone to plead so fervently, but she knew of nothing else to do except listen.

"Is it like the *tezlitac* said?" petitioned Rentería. "There's no help for me except . . . to die?"

Yes! Dru cried silently. That was it — she wanted him to die!

A Siwash. That's all he was.

The word bounced around in Jake's head

as he kept his nodding Appaloosa at the hindquarter of Nub's sorrel. The five horses had carried the riders far enough from the storm's swath for the bandits' trail to show again, and now the foreman led the way on south through endless creosote marked by ocotillo and rustling yucca stalks.

The two men had barely spoken since Jake's angry remarks the day before, but only in the past hour had Jake realized how much Nub was to blame for the girls' abduction. If he and Dru hadn't arranged for everyone to meet at the Cross C's so they could try to win approval, she would have celebrated Christmas at home in Marfa with Ruthie and Annie. Jake would have been there as well, and the raid on the Cross C's would have happened without them.

Now, more than ever, Jake bristled at the thought of his daughter in Nub's arms. She deserved better, not this damned Indian who stirred up so many bad memories of things Jake could never change.

The two of them were far enough ahead of the others so that Jake could talk freely.

"You ever touch my daughter?"

Nub turned as Jake took his Appaloosa abreast on the sorrel's right. "Sir?"

"My girl. You ever touch her?"

The foreman looked uncomfortable, but

Jake couldn't tell if it was from guilt or embarrassment.

"I've already indicated," said Nub, "that I respect Dru above anyone."

"Answer the damned question."

"We embrace, Mr. Graves, if that's the nature of your inquiry."

"It ain't," snapped Jake, "and I figure you know it."

"Sir, I would never do anything to jeopardize your daughter's reputation."

"Reputation, hell! She's a white girl, and here you been slippin' around seein' her."

"I love Dru, Mr. Graves. I would exchange my life for hers a dozen times over. And no, sir, by your definition, I have never touched her."

Jake snorted. "I better not ever find out different."

A little ashamed that he had caused such a scene, Jake urged his horse ahead, throwing dust back across his would-be son-in-law.

On through the morning, Jake rode in silence, his regret building for picking a fight that no one needed. He was glad Annie hadn't been around to witness it, for he had done exactly what she had warned against upon telling him of the marriage plans. Anyway, laying the responsibility on Nub for all of this was probably unfair. By the same logic, Jake could as easily have blamed himself; if he hadn't been so set in his thinking, Dru would have revealed the relationship earlier rather than drawing everyone together at the Cross C's.

A time or two, Jake started to drop back and apologize to Nub, but he was too stubborn to do anything but sulk and let his Appaloosa carry him on through the cholla and creosote. Behind him, meanwhile, he heard Bill Ike repeatedly try to mend things with Bo.

"We caught hell, didn't we, boy? Never seen a storm like it."

Bo gave no response.

"Wished I'd've been back there with you," Bill Ike went on. "Guess nobody ever told you how to get under your saddle."

Still, there were only hoofbeats and the rattle of saddles, but Bill Ike was undeterred.

"Beat you up bad, that hail did. Soon's we stop, I'll slice open a pear pad and fix you up that poultice you was wantin' 'fore daylight."

But the younger Capps stayed sullen. Jake supposed it was to be expected that situations like this would give rise to foul moods.

Midday found the riders bunched closely

behind Jake as he neared a squalid *jacal* set against a creosote-infested hill near the Rio Grande. A few minutes ago, he had passed an abandoned goatherd hut, but this mud-daubed dwelling with a collapsing rock front showed signs of occupancy. Chimney smoke curled over the large boulder in back, and a small winter garden to the side seemed well-tended.

"Santa Maria, this place . . ."

Alfonso struggled for words as Jake looked back and found the *muchacho* wide-eyed astride the chestnut.

"*Mi papá* bring me here from up *río. Señora* Sabana live this *jacal.* She a *curandera. Tezlitac,* too."

"*Tezlitac,* Alfonso?" repeated Nub. "A type of *bruja,* witch?"

"*Señora* Sabana stronger than *bruja.* When Jesús Rentería the *tlahuelpuchi* kill my sister, we bring *tezlitac* home with us to drive evil away."

"Wet's jabberin' away again, ain't he, boy?" Bill Ike addressed his son.

Bo had nothing to say, but the *muchacho* went on to describe a ritual the *tezlitac* had conducted in the room where his sister had died. Jake still figured the baby's bruising and blue skin for signs of cholera, but no one was going to convince Alfonso of it. His voice was that of someone certain that an agent of evil was responsible.

Señora Sabana had placed a slanting cross of pine in the room's center and laid the baby's naked body on it. At the feet, the *tezlitac* allowed a small bronze censer to burn hot with resin. Taking it up by its chains, she walked clockwise around the cross. She spread the incense in this manner three times before repeating the process in the opposite direction. All the while, she called upon Catholic saints and the mountain spirits of Tlaxcala.

Returning the censer to its place, the *tezlitac* had prayed to God and Our Lady of Guadalupe while cleaning the body three times with bunched capulin branches, the stems of the herb ocoxochitl, and dried agave roots.

Bill Ike's mockery had reached new heights by now, and Jake himself had heard all he wanted. Nevertheless, Alfonso wasn't finished. As the *muchacho* grew emotional, Jake was respectful enough to turn in the saddle and face him.

"*Mi mamá* stand against wall with arms out like cross all this time," Alfonso related. "*Tezlitac* clean her like my sister, and then Mama kiss foot of cross. When *Señora* Sabana sweep walls same way, door too, evil all gone."

The boy's eyes narrowed in a way that Jake could understand.

"But *mi hermana,* my sister, still dead," said Alfonso, his eyes glistening. He gripped the handle of his sheathed machete and gritted his teeth. "When I find Rentería the *tlahuelpuchi,* he die too."

The *muchacho* would have to stand in line for his chance, thought Jake.

Thirty yards shy of the *jacal's* open door, Jake veered right with the bandits' trail and pulled rein beside scrub mesquites. The soil under his Appaloosa's breast was agitated, evidence of hitching, and as Jake lifted his gaze he saw more tracks. Eight horsemen had ridden in, and eight had ridden out, bearing downriver past the *jacal's* far corner.

But before leaving this place, several had entered the home of the *curandera* and *tezlitac.*

Nub had taken his horse a few yards down the trail leading away, and Jake watched him lean off the sorrel in inspection.

"These hoofprints are significantly fresher than the ones approaching here," said the foreman, tracing their course with his hand.

Jake studied the *jacal* where the riders must have spent a lot of time. He remembered the signs of the horse wreck in the

205

poison-tipped *lechuguilla,* and he worried that one of the girls might have needed this healer. Climbing off his horse, he secured the reins and started for the door.

"I go with you, *señor,*" Alfonso said from behind.

Just as Jake passed Nub's sorrel, the foreman turned.

"We're closing rapidly, Mr. Graves. I'll persist in the chase rather than linger."

Lingering? Was that what the Indian thought he was doing?

Wagging his head, Jake didn't break stride. He was vaguely aware that Bill Ike and his son rode on with Nub, but right now he was focused on what he might learn inside the *jacal.* Nearing, he smelled an unusual odor and heard someone praying, and when he reached the door a wavering voice spoke from the shadows.

"Wait."

Jake stopped and the voice took up its prayer again. As his eyes began to adjust, he saw a hunched little woman slowly circling a slanted wood cross on the earthen floor. With each step, she dangled a smoking censer back and forth to spread incense.

"She drive away evil!" whispered Alfonso. "*Tlahuelpuchi* go inside!"

Jake was in a hurry, but for long minutes

he watched the ritual play out as the *muchacho* had described. It ended with the old woman brushing the jambs and door head with a handful of herb stems and branches, and now the two of them stood face-to-face.

"Two girls been here? Bunch of men?" Jake asked.

He watched the movement of her pinched eyes as she looked him up and down.

"*Estas con ellos?* You with them?"

"They taken my daughter and niece. We come after 'em. One's got dark hair and the other's fair-headed."

Tilting her head, the woman peered around Jake's shoulder. "*¿Quien es éste?*"

Jake glanced back at Alfonso. "Just a boy ridin' with us."

"You come to *mi casa* up *río*," said the *muchacho*. "You drive evil away. My sister die *chupado por el brujo,* sucked by the witch."

"*Sí, tlahuelpuchi.*" Rage began to build in the woman's wrinkled face, her lips tightening and her brows dropping. When she repeated "*Tlahuelpuchi!*" it was like an oath, and she turned, mumbling to herself, and stalked around in the shadows. When she returned and faced Jake, her eyes bulged.

"*Tlahuelpuchi!*" she said again.

Seeing her conviction, Jake wondered if

Nub had been right about there being things of which a man couldn't even dream.

"Them girls," he repeated. "You seen them?"

At last, the hunched woman was able to answer. "*Sí,* one very sick with fever."

"You help her any? Which one was it?"

"Yellow-haired *señorita.* I used ways of ancestors."

"She doin' all right?"

"They put her on *caballo* and take her away. Maybe she better now. *Quien sabe,* who knows?"

"The dark-haired girl," said Jake. "What about her?"

"She tell me *hombres* take them. She want me to help."

Jake looked over her shoulder and checked the shadows again. "You by yourself? Nothin' you could do, I don't guess."

"No, *señor.*"

Rasping his hand across his bristly face, Jake looked downriver at the tracks that disappeared around the *jacal.* He still had another question, one that haunted him, but he didn't know if he had the courage to ask.

"They . . . They treatin' them good? The girls been . . . ?"

Violated. Outraged. Raped. No matter the

word, he just couldn't say it. He turned, afraid to read the *curandera's* answer in her features.

"*¿Quien sabe?*" she said again. "I tell her no *señorita* safe with *tlahuelpuchi.* He drink the blood every month."

God A'mighty. It had been alarming enough to hear that kind of talk from a *muchacho* like Alfonso who would believe anything. But to hear it from the old *curandera* and see the conviction in her eyes made Jake's skin crawl.

He spun on his heel and brushed past the *muchacho.* "We got to go."

Rushing to his horse, Jake mounted up and turned the bronc into the tracks leading away. He had just come abreast of the doorway when a quaking *"un momento"* caused him to hold the Appaloosa and face the *curandera.* She came out a short distance, a bent wisp of a woman raising dust with her shuffling steps.

"One thing nobody know," said the *curandera.* "I tell her before they go."

"Told my daughter what?" pressed Jake, impatient to strike out. "Hurry up — they's two lives at stake."

"Three," said the *curandera.* "She is going to be a mother."

Jake touched spurs to horsehide and the

Appaloosa was away, the rising hoofbeats lost among seven powerful words about Dru and the Siwash.

CHAPTER 12

The place where Consuela's blood had run.

Hidden away in the tall cane and catclaw bushes near the *río,* the small clearing marked by a drooping black willow had been a portal to hell. From it must have risen Consuela-who-couldn't-be-Consuela, a devil sent to torment, and now the blood place was drawing Rentería closer with every pace of his black. He just didn't know to what end.

Once there, would the devil twin release him? Or had the *tezlitac* been right, and his only hope was to die?

Either way, he wouldn't find out unless he eluded the men who followed.

All the way from the *jacal,* Rentería and his command had pressed the horses. In flood-prone bottomland, they had navigated thick devil weed and broken through ten-foot stands of rustling cane. Worst had been the claws of huisache acacia and the spines hidden in the green branches of needle-leafed paloverde trees.

Where a range of imposing crags came out of the northeast and pushed against the *río,* Rentería was forced to take the riders out of the jungled bottom. In the creosote desert, he struck an eroded burro trail and followed it as it climbed, narrow and rocky, toward a jagged notch in the serrated summit cliffs. Small boulders lined the way, sometimes supporting prickly pear or lechuguilla that pricked his leg as the black listed with the slippage of its hoofs.

Looking back, down and away past the devil twin swaying in the saddle, Rentería saw the *río.* It unfurled peacefully to the north-northwest, a silvery ribbon between the dark bands of the floodplain. Suddenly, no more than a mile distant, light flashed from the dense growth along the bank.

He held his black and saw it flash again, and he looked at Consuela-who-wasn't-Consuela and knew the price he had paid for lingering at the *jacal* for her *amiga.* Turning, he ordered the *hombre* ahead to hurry, but there was only so much a horse could do on a trail so rugged.

No matter the effigy Rentería had carved or the death spell he had cast, the pursuers had almost ridden them down. He had appealed to the *tezlitac* and watched the storm clouds gather, and had even begged the favor of *el diablo* and felt the ground shake. And yet they were there in the brush, riders with firearms that glinted in the sun.

As soon as Rentería and his command reached the V in the sawtooth cliffs, he weighed his options. He may have believed himself a *tlahuelpuchi* with *brujería* powers, but he was also a soldier, and what couldn't be done with witchcraft, he would accomplish with generalship.

The windy gap was only yards wide and marked by a big Spanish dagger. The bluff on the right was impossibly steep and unstable, while its sister peak was at least manageable, despite angling sharply up and away. Where there was sufficient soil in the lower reach, pitaya and cacti had taken root, giving it a smattering of green. But above was only boulder piled upon boulder, one hundred or more feet, the sunlit heights almost white against the blue sky.

Signaling a halt, Rentería dispatched an *hombre* to scramble up and reconnoiter toward the river. The lofty hogback cut by the pass was like a razor's edge, and Rentería took his horse only a few paces farther before the trail fell away on the far side. Over his horse's tousled mane, he looked down past a scattering of modest boulders on the slope at a yucca-dotted basin rimmed by abrupt bluffs. A little over a carbine shot across, with access limited to a steep trail in and out, the hollow was more than Rentería could have hoped for.

"*¡Tres hombres!*" the scout called down.

Rentería looked back, encouraged. *Three, not five.* He would end this chase, and soon, and in another day or so he would be back at the blood place and maybe find peace.

"Already told this to Graves, but I'm countin' on you to put in a good word with that little girl's folks."

Bill Ike had relaxed his efforts to get a response from Bo, who rode point just ahead of him. Nor was Nub, from his position behind the two, anxious to talk with the grasping old devil. But as their three horses dropped single-file from a hogback pass toward a basin surrounded by bluffs, Bill Ike persisted.

"Foreman? You back there still?" He checked as his bay's hoofs slipped and slid down between small boulders. "I was sayin' how good it'd be if you's to tell your boss what all Bo's did for that daughter of his."

Around the bay's white hind leg, Nub saw Bo shoot a quick look back.

"May I ask," countered Nub with a sharp breath, "what courtesies your son extended her?"

Bo began to squirm in the saddle.

"Ain't many men," said Bill Ike, "would do for her what my boy done."

A boy, Bill Ike called him. A damned cur was more appropriate.

"Share specifics with us, Bo," goaded Nub. He was through with granting the man a title of respect. "Proceed with briefing us on what you did for Miss Ruthie."

But Bill Ike replied instead. "W'y, all this chasin' and stuff."

Nub stayed focused on the younger man. "Might you wish to augment his statement, Bo?"

Bill Ike seemed confused, and he scratched his goatee as he twisted from one of them to the other. "Somethin' you two's holdin' back?"

"Bo, inform your father, why don't you?" Nub continued. "Then he can personally apprise Mr. Graves upon his return."

Bill Ike clearly wanted to gain a place in Nub's good graces; winning the favor of the Cross C owners for Bo was too important not to try. But when it came to the scoundrel's prejudices, even greed must have had its limits.

"What's with all the 'Bo this' and 'Bo that,' foreman?" Bill Ike challenged. "That's *Mister* Bo, or *Mister* Capps. These parts, you show respect to a white man."

"Respect," Nub repeated. "Care to inquire of your son his position on respect?"

Bill Ike pulled rein and turned in the saddle, his brows beetling. He was ready for a fight. "Now, listen here, you —"

"Quit it, Bill Ike."

Nub wasn't surprised when Ruthie's suitor interjected himself into the matter, but Bill Ike obviously was. His jaw muscles were already relaxing as he turned away to Bo.

"Well!" said Bill Ike. "See you's talkin' to your ol' daddy again. Just remindin' him of his place, is all. He don't have no right to —"

"I don't want to hear any more." Bo's blazed-face roan had veered right with a switchback to avoid a small boulder, and he held the horse and faced the older man.

"Just takin' up for you, boy," said Bill Ike. "What the hell's he tryin' to bait you about?"

"Between him and me."

"Your count is inaccurate," spoke up Nub. "There's a third party involved. No, more than that — her parents as well."

Bill Ike suddenly seemed worried, judging by his glances front and back. "Boy, you done somethin' to aggravate that girl's folks?"

"We get Ruthie back and they won't matter," said Bo.

"They's just the chance we need to get somewheres. Don't you go throwin' it away."

"That all you think about, Bill Ike?" Abruptly, Bo's voice had the same confrontational tone that Nub had overheard at daybreak. "Be nice if you worried about somebody 'sides yourself. I'm hurting all over still."

"Now, don't go gettin' riled up like this mornin'. You always *was* one for fallin' to pieces over some little somethin'. Your ol' daddy here's just —"

"Yeah, I know *exactly* what you are. I marry into the Cross C's, I just might cut my old daddy out altogether."

"Aw, you don't mean that."

But Bo didn't respond. He urged his horse on down toward the basin, and he wouldn't look back even as Bill Ike called after him.

At bottom, they struck a flat with good soil. More than a hundred yards wide, it supported big Spanish daggers interspersed with a few modest boulders. Nature had formed a bowl here, a valley secreted away and secured by the ridge behind and sharply rising bluffs elsewhere. Only at ten o'clock was there a break, a small canyon that drained this den of danger.

Maybe some inherited Apache instinct spoke to Nub, because despite the tempting beauty, that's how he thought of the place — a den of danger. The walls hemming him in were too much like the jaws of a wolf trap ready to spring, and he wished the men in front would hurry their horses to the whitewashed trail that angled left-to-right up the steep bluff ahead.

Its rock summit strangely drew Nub's attention, and he gripped his shotgun; maybe his Mescalero forebears spoke again. He and the Cappses were halfway across, his sorrel nodding along between an isolated boulder on the animal's right flank and a forked Spanish dagger ahead. Suddenly from the rim burst fire — the unmistakable flash of a muzzle — and even as dirt exploded in front of Nub and the valley roared, another flash showed, and another and another.

"They's on us!" yelled Bill Ike.

The sorrel went wild, and Nub was in no position to do anything but step off with a half twist and let the animal bolt. He dived for the boulder, a lichen-stained mass three feet in diameter. Rolling, he came up with his cheek against rock and took a bead around the hewn edge. The rim was fifty yards away and eighty feet up, beyond killing range for his shotgun, but he could still spray the shooters with .33-caliber pellets.

His Stevens boomed, the butt plate recoiling hard against his shoulder. But even before he could pump another shell into the chamber, a rifle cracked from behind and rock shards caught his hat brim. The ricochet whizzed through yucca as he spun, finding a glinting rifle high on the crag over the pass. To another report, dirt kicked up an arm's length from Nub, and all he could do was scramble around the boulder in search of cover.

As bullets flew, he found a protected place and drew up his legs. With rock breaking apart left and right, he scrunched his shoulders, but he knew that a shooter would only have to slide along the bluff to catch him squarely down the sights.

Caught in a cross fire, Nub couldn't even shoot back, and Bill Ike and Bo must have been similarly pinned considering their exchange.

"Do something, Bill Ike!" yelled Bo.

"Horse got off with my gun! All three's run down in that little canyon. Got your six-shooter?"

"They're too far away!"

"Pepper their butts anyhow!"

"Can't, Bill Ike! Shooting all around me!"

"I-god, shoot up in the air if you got to. Let 'em know they can't rush us!"

A quick revolver shot ensued, a deterrence round that wouldn't be enough. Bill Ike followed up by cursing the bandits at the top of his lungs, and if invectives had been bullets, he could have routed the entire Carrancista army. But while Bill Ike was swearing, Nub was planning.

Death was upon him, and if his demise would have affected no one else, he could have accepted it, confident in what lay beyond. But Dru and Ruthie were in the hands of devils, and if he didn't do something soon, he would seal their living hell. He couldn't bear the thought of such a fate for Ruthie, but a fever burned inside him when he considered Dru.

The next instant, Nub was up and sprinting through gunfire, expecting to catch a slug with every step. Ruthie, he respected and felt obligated to protect. But Dru was as much a cause worth dying for as living for, and if this was how Nub was to meet his end, he would do so proudly.

He bore toward the right side of the basin,

for there was a black rock ahead in the yucca. The bullets chased at his heels, but he made it across to a momentary place of shelter. Dirt from a near miss sprinkled his boot, and when another one fractured the rock at his elbow, he broke into the open again. Seconds earlier he had scouted toward the pass, and he knew where another boulder lay.

Nub zigzagged back across the valley this way, somehow dodging the gunfire. As he neared the slope under the high pass, the puffs of dirt couldn't keep pace and stopped; he was out of effective range for rifles on the bluff. But the marksman on the crag above Nub could shoot down from closer quarters now, a situation that still threatened to make every breath Nub's last.

He gained the slope and pushed up it, weaving from rock to rock as bullets danced at his feet and ricocheted. On hope and a prayer he climbed, a desperate man giving his all for a greater purpose. He clambered across switchbacks in the trail and reached the base of the summit cliffs to the right of the pass, but not until he threw himself under a bulge in the rock did he have a measure of security.

He lay writhing beside the lichen-covered limestone, his chest heaving and the underlying rubble grating his cheek. He didn't think it possible to hear his own heart labor, but its frantic pounding was unmistakable against the gunfire across the valley.

When he recovered, he stood and checked the rock for handholds. It was not a uniform face but rather boulder stacked upon boulder, and he edged left and found a dark crack angling up to disappear over the pitch's curving contour. He worked a boot into the crevice and climbed, a challenge with a shotgun in his hand. Twice, he almost turned back, but he reminded himself why he was here and he found strength he didn't know he had.

Twenty feet up, he crawled onto a secluded nook where towering rocks intersected. The face ahead was sheer, but the pitch on his right stairstepped up a yard at a time, the successive levels holding enough soil for pincushion cacti.

With his twelve-gauge ready, Nub went higher. There was a marksman up there, concealed in the rocks outlined against the sky, and the bandit's rifle was the key to the assault below. Any moment, cross fire would flush the Cappses, and they wouldn't be as lucky as Nub. They would die, and he and Jake and a boy with a machete would be the only ones left against a force of six.

As Nub reached over his head for what might have been a wraparound ledge, the rifle boomed from nearby, the report rolling through the boulders and echoing across the valley. The uproar made it impossible to pinpoint the shooter. But as instinct drew Nub's gaze above his left shoulder, a voice from the past whispered to him.

Someone is there. Just a few feet up, hidden by the rock, someone is waiting.

Nub froze, his shotgun poised to kill.

CHAPTER 13

Even as the *curandera's* words tormented him, Jake saw himself in Alfonso.

They rode downriver, Jake's Appaloosa a horse length ahead of the *muchacho's* chestnut, and for miles Alfonso had talked of nothing but Rentería's role in the loss of his family. Now, revenge dominated the boy's words.

"He kill *mi hermana,* he kill *mi mamá,* he kill *mi papá.* Now I kill *tlahuelpuchi*!"

He said it again and again as if it were a muted war cry, and when he wasn't repeating it, he was describing in detail how he would go about it.

"He on ground, dead but not dead. Eyes look up, evil eyes, *diablo* eyes. I take shoulders. I roll him, face in dirt. Sun bright in machete. I chop neck. I chop and chop for *mi hermana, mi mamá, mi papá.* Head gone, *tlahuelpuchi* gone."

It was the kind of obsession that Jake

recognized, because it had been his own for forty-seven years.

It was startling insight into himself, seeing this fixation on unfulfilled vengeance play out in someone else. Every time Jake glanced back he found a face that no sixteen-year-old should have — an intense face so sad and pained. He wondered if, in the darkest of moments in Mason County, his own features had been this wrenched when his mother had begged him to let the Lord take away his hurt.

Jake turned to the *muchacho,* understanding him as never before.

"Say you do all this. Say you go and kill him like you say. That be enough?"

"*¿Que?*"

"It be over and done with?" Jake asked. "Or will you still be lettin' ever'thing gnaw at you, time you're my age?"

From Alfonso's expression, it was clear that he didn't understand.

"Just do what you got to and let it go somehow," said Jake. "You don't want it eatin' you up your whole life like me."

"Something it happen?"

"Kind of like you, I guess. Lost a sister bad. When I was your age, somebody used to tell me what I oughta do. You know, to put it behind me."

"How they say, *Señor* Jake?"

"Funny how it sticks with me, what my mother kept tellin'. I run off and left her, but ever' so often I still hear her readin' it to me. 'Humble yourselves in the sight of the Lord, and he shall lift you up.' Like an eagle flyin', she'd say."

He pulled rein and so did Alfonso, and as they faced one another, Jake relived in the *muchacho's* eyes all the troubled decades since Mason County.

"Hope you can do what I never could," said Jake.

He rode on, but too many things rode with him. What he had seen down the barrel of the Sharp's carbine a lifetime ago controlled him today more than ever.

Indians. Animals. Soulless devils.

The painted riders out of hell had carried his sister away and violated her, and now, forcibly or not, the same thing had happened to his daughter. At sixteen, Jake had just let it happen. This time, he would make sure that no damned Siwash ever again touched somebody he loved.

Jake heard the gunshots as he and Alfonso neared the gap high in the serrated cliffs.

The reports seemed to come from above the pass, maybe from the left-side crag shining in the sun. The pattern of gunfire suggested a single carbine, for the shots were never closer together than five seconds, the minimum time necessary to lever in a fresh cartridge and take aim. Circumstances and instinct told Jake that Nub and the Cappses had been caught in an ambush, and he dismounted a few hundred yards below the cliffs and handed the Appaloosa's reins to Alfonso.

"Stay with the horses," he told the *muchacho.*

Fixing his gaze on the gap, the greatest blight in the burnished heights, Jake climbed with a Marlin carbine rammed full with .44 Special rounds.

The rocky trail, snaking against the steep rise, led him up through lechuguilla and prickly pear, and he continued to hear only a lone carbine until a Spanish dagger rose up the notch ahead. From beyond, he could distinguish more gunfire, faint but growing louder with his every crouching step. Assessing the situation, Jake understood — from high on the left-side peak, a sniper played a deadly role in an attack across the hogback.

Even as Jake gained the yucca in the narrow pass and reconnoitered, the rocky heights still hid the shooter. But the bandit's gunfire persisted, each crack echoing through the gap. No matter how daunting the prospect, Jake started up after him, testing his sixty-three years against boulder after boulder that reached into the overhead sky.

It wasn't easy, fighting age and the effects of three days of hell, but he climbed higher and higher as the wind moaned between rocks. Suddenly, as he planted a knee on a ledge in the upper reaches, he heard the click-click of a carbine lever.

He was a dead man as he came up with his Marlin, but even when the other carbine boomed as if from point-blank range, Jake had a reprieve, for he was unharmed and there was no shooter in sight. Searching, he swept the muzzle of his weapon across a twelve-foot wall in his face, and then left over the rim of a cliff and right toward a point a few yards away where a squared boulder stood waist-high against the distance. The hogback played tricks with sound, but the abrupt drag of iron across rock from just over the boulder was no echo.

Somebody was there, the *shooter* was there, and Jake gained his feet and moved in for the kill.

All of his pent-up hatred — not only for the bandits and those long-ago Indians, but also for himself — rose up in an instant. It brought with it a rage he had never known before, and his finger had already begun squeezing the trigger as he threw himself across the boulder and looked down over the barrel of his Marlin.

Good God!

He peered into a twelve-gauge bore, the shotgun behind it glinting in the sun. Pinched against the stock was Nub's up-turned face, backdropped by rocks thirty feet below. For a split second, eternity for both men hinged on the twitch of forefingers, and then the shotgun barrel slid a few inches to the side and roared.

What the hell!

Jake rolled away, too shaken to process the fact that he was still alive. Nub was saying something, for his lips moved as he looked past Jake. Momentarily deafened, Jake twisted around to the sheer wall above and saw a bandit pitch out of the sky. The man looked dead as he glanced off the ledge, but there was no doubt after the body plunged another forty feet to the rocks.

Scrambling to his feet, Jake reconnoitered a valley off the far side of the hogback. From here, he could see everything: two bandits firing from the far bluff, two more charging their horses across the basin, dirt exploding around boulders halfway across.

Throwing his carbine against his shoulder, Jake fired at the lead rider, and then levered in another cartridge and fired again. The second shot knocked the bandit from his horse, and the tide of battle changed.

The other horseman reined up in obvious confusion, and he stayed in place long enough for Jake's third shot to send his sombrero flying. Now the Mexican wheeled his animal and fled, but Jake chased him all the way up the far trail with .44 Special slugs. At top, the Mexican was out of range, and so were the shooters on the rim and three other figures farther back with horses, but soon they were all mounted and raising dust in the distance.

Jake's carbine had snapped against an empty chamber with his last attempted shot, but he wasn't finished. Reaching across his chest, he drew his Colt revolver from his shoulder holster and turned.

Before him stood Nub, casually cradling the twelve-gauge, and Jake drove the .45 muzzle between the Indian's dark eyes.

"You son of a bitch!"

His ears still ringing, Jake could barely hear his own voice. But he had no trouble discerning the confusion in Nub's face, or reading on the man's lips what his damaged ears couldn't make out.

"Sir, he would have killed you," Nub said calmly. "Had I not fired when I did, he would have killed you."

With a rage greater than ever, Jake thumbed back the hammer. "What you done to my daughter . . . !"

"What *about* Dru?"

"Least be man enough to own up to it!"

"Sir, I assure you I don't grasp your meaning."

Jake snorted. "Lie to me, why don't you!" The .45 shook in his hand. "Just like you lied before!"

Even in the face of a cocked six-shooter, Nub never averted his eyes. "When was I untruthful with you, Mr. Graves? I —"

"You said you never did touch her, you damned Siwash!"

"Only in the sense I explained. Why would you think otherwise?"

Jake's finger stayed firm against the trigger. "Never do nothin' to hurt her reputation, you tell me. And all the time she's carryin' your baby!"

"My — ?" For long seconds, Nub seemed unable to find words. "That's not accurate. It cannot be accurate."

"You sayin' it's somebody else's? You makin' out now my daughter's a whore?"

"No, sir, I am not. Were you to search the world over, you would never find anyone as virtuous. I cannot imagine who would tell you such a thing, but you couldn't be more mistaken."

"So she ain't with child?"

"No, sir. As God is my judge, I swear it. Whoever tarnished her reputation will have to answer to me."

Nub said it with such conviction that Jake questioned whether he should have leveled such an accusation. Hell, hadn't he been a law enforcement officer all these decades? Since when did he pass sentence on someone on the basis of such flimsy evidence as the old *curandera's* remark?

Lowering the six-shooter, Jake took it off full cock and started away. But Nub's words wouldn't let him leave.

"I misjudged your character, Mr. Graves."

Facing Nub again, Jake listened in silence.

"At times our mission has seemed hopeless," continued Nub, "and the strain is wearing on us. But what you did went beyond the pale. Even if the allegation were true, any man who would consider killing his own grandchild's father isn't worthy of my respect."

Turning, Nub lowered himself off the rim

and dropped out of sight, leaving Jake to dwell on all that the younger man had said.

CHAPTER 14

Even as Rentería pushed the pace of the horses, Dru rode with renewed hope.

The gunfire from across the valley had done more than throw a scare into him. His command of five had been cut almost in half, and the remaining three riders seemed as concerned as he as they looked back through the billowing dust. There were men back there somewhere, determined men hidden by the folds of the land, and Dru knew they were coming for Ruthie and her.

Held at a distance from the skirmish, Dru hadn't been able to identify the pursuers. But as buoyed as she was by the thought of who might be with them, she was just as stricken by fear. Bullets had flown across that valley, and the vermin who had fired the weapons hadn't cared how many decent men they might kill.

Oh, God! she cried silently. *Please let Nub and Dad be all right!*

As the miles passed under the hoofs, the two of them seemed a constant presence, but the *curandera's* startling news about Ruthie also vied for a place in her thoughts. There was another matter as well, one that Dru had almost forgotten in all that had happened, but now the old woman's strange remarks about *tlahuelpuchi,* or some such term, came back as Dru's dun maintained a jog trot behind Rentería.

The *curandera* had virtually spat the word at the *capitán* as he had run from the *jacal,* but she had also shouted a warning to Dru before the riders had rushed Ruthie and her away on their horses. Now, Dru tried to make sense of it, something about blood and danger. How had the stooped little woman phrased it? That *tlahuelpuchi* had to drink human blood every month or die, and that she and Ruthie might be next?

Numbed by the constant threats of the last three days, Dru didn't have an ounce of fear left to devote to any new peril, but the *curandera's* assertion about Rentería might explain some things. Ever since the skirmish, he had ridden like a man dying. Hunched, his shoulders bent, he seemed drained in body and spirit — a toll beyond all expectation. Exhaustion, Dru could understand, but for the last hour he had also glanced back at the two of them with strange desire. It wasn't the leer that Dru had come to expect from his men, but something more, something ungodly.

There seemed to be hunger in it, or thirst, a craving that made Dru long for even the pure evil his face had presented when she had first seen him up close.

Despite the hard ride, Ruthie had improved throughout the day, and she, too, noticed the change in Rentería, for she came abreast of Dru when the trail allowed and posed a quiet question.

"How come him lookin' at us so funny?"

Dru didn't want to alarm her more than she already was. "He's always acted odd around me."

"He's scared of you, Dru, like I been sayin'. But this is somethin' different."

Ruthie glanced at Rentería and her voice dropped to a hush, even though the *capitán* didn't speak English.

"That old woman back there. All like a dream, kind of. That funny-soundin' word she called him when we was leavin' . . . That really happen? She make out like he was one of those Mex'can vampires?"

"You've heard of them?" Dru asked with surprise.

"Remember Mama visitin' kinfolk in

Rhode Island? She came back tellin' about a vampire scare there in the early nineties. Alfonso heard us talkin' and told us about the Mex'can kind. Starts with a *T-L,* I think."

"Ruthie, you don't really think there's such a thing, do you?"

"So she did call him that?"

"*Tlahuelpuchi,* I think."

"That's it, *tlahuelpuchi.* Alfonso was goin' on about it killin' his whole family."

Dru felt a chill, and she checked Rentería's slumping figure as he rocked with his horse's jog trot.

"Mexicans are just superstitious, Dad says," Dru reminded herself out loud. "Always laying blame elsewhere for things that happen naturally."

"Maybe so, but I didn't sleep that night after Alfonso's tellin'."

Rentería glanced back at them again, the same alarming desire in his features.

"I-I don't like this, Dru," Ruthie added. "The way he keeps lookin' at us . . . What-what if he *is* one of those things?"

"He's just a man, Ruthie. That's all he *can* be — just a wicked, wicked man."

"Alfonso says they go lookin' for blood ever' month. They get ready by buildin' a fire out of agave roots and go to chantin' over it. They'll walk across it three times, makin' a cross, and then plop down in it. Instead of it burnin', it lets them change into somethin' else. Their legs fall off and they go out huntin' for blood lookin' like a buzzard or coyote or somethin'."

"That's silly, Ruthie. Just plain silly."

Ruthie's nerves were getting the best of her, and Dru could see it in her paling face and hear it in her rapid-fire voice.

"I don't know, Dru — I don't know — I don't know."

"Ruthie, you need to —"

"I want out of this, Dru! I just want to go back — me and Bo, that's all I want!"

"You've got to hang on. Both of us have got to. Don't do something foolish again."

"When's it goin' to end? The vampires and filthy — what are we goin' to do!"

"Listen to me, Ruthie. They're coming to get us. Those men back there, they'll catch up again and all this will be over with. Bo might even be with them, him and Dad and Nub."

Nub! Now it was Dru who became emotional, and she looked away, her eyes stinging.

"You think so?" asked Ruthie. "You really think Bo's found out and he's comin' for me?"

Dru didn't want to spread false hope; from what she had heard of Bo Capps, he wasn't any more reliable than his father. But she supposed that false hope was better than none at all.

"He could be, Ruthie. He could be back there just out of sight."

Dru turned and found her cousin looking back, searching through the pluming dust.

"You really care about him, don't you," said Dru.

Ruthie faced her. "Him and me's gettin' married — I tell you that?"

Married! To Bo Capps?

"Ruthie, you told me you had a big secret, but I had no idea."

Remembering what the *curandera* had said about Ruthie, Dru wondered again if her cousin had an even bigger secret. She wasn't showing yet, but why else would she marry someone like him?

"I swan, Ruthie," Dru added. "Bo Capps."

"Soon's Mama and Daddy get back, Bo and me's talkin' it over with them."

In some ways, Ruthie's father was a lot like Dru's: opinionated and set in his ways. That would be one conversation Dru would be glad to miss.

"How you think they'll take it, you be-ing . . ." Not knowing her condition for sure, Dru didn't say more.

The mention of Bo had clearly had a calming effect on Ruthie, and now there was promise and anticipation in her features.

"I'm callin' him Little Bo," she said. She even had a trace of a smile. "That's a good name, don't you think? Beauregard Capps Junior?"

Despite all the clues, Dru was nonetheless taken aback.

"You . . . You okay with this, Ruthie?" she asked.

"Oh, people would talk if they found out. Mama and Daddy too, but we're not tellin' them. We'll get married quick and they won't think nothin' of it, the baby comin' early and all."

"So they won't have a problem with . . ." Again, Dru caught herself.

"With Bo?" completed Ruthie. "If they do, we'll run off to El Paso and get married. We come back and Mama will have a grandbaby to spoil and Bo can be the son she never did have."

"She's not the one I'd worry about."

"Oh, Daddy will come around. I know Bo's got his faults, drinkin' and all. But Mama says Daddy did too when he was younger. She straightened him out, and so can I with Bo. He stops drinkin' and he'll

240

change ever' which way. Be more dependable and not so selfish and start thinkin'
before doin'."

"That's a lot to work on, Ruthie."

"So how's Beauregard Capps Junior
sound, Dru? Don't it sound high-class, like
one of Daddy's prize bulls?"

Ruthie began to giggle — remarkably,
considering the circumstances — and Dru
got caught up in the moment.

"The very idea, Ruthie Cowan!" she
exclaimed. "Comparing Little Bo to a
Hereford bull!"

Maybe they both needed to laugh, and for
an instant Dru even forgot about their dire
plight. Then Rentería again made brief eye
contact, his strange desire stronger than
ever, and Dru's shoulders shook from a
shudder rather than laughter.

Rentería's glance dispirited Ruthie as well.
"See the way he looks at us, Dru? He's got
to be a *tlahuelpuchi*!"

Ruthie spoke the word louder than before
— too loudly, and Rentería clearly overheard. Confronting him was the last thing
Dru would have wanted, and she didn't
know what to expect when he reined up and
wheeled his animal, forcing the two of them
to stop.

"Why she say *tlahuelpuchi*?" he asked Dru.

His voice was lifeless, and Dru just looked at him, not knowing how to answer.

With a wave of his arm, Rentería ordered his men to withdraw. Once they were out of earshot, he took his horse abreast of hers so that they faced one another.

"Tell me, Consuela," he begged.

"It was the *curandera* that said it," she managed. "She told you that at the door."

"It's not my fault, Consuela. *Lo siento,* it's not my fault!"

Anguish twisted his face, but there was also that troubling craving.

"I protected you, *mi hermana,*" he continued. "Every night I watched over you to keep *tlahuelpuchi* away! *Ay Dios,* what I did to help you until . . ."

For a moment, the indefinable craving in his features had gone away, but now it came back, more troubling than ever. His gaze darted to the side, as if drawn by Ruthie, and then it returned, only to shift again. The pattern persisted, as if he were at the mercy of something that drove him to choose between the two of them.

Maybe Dru had been wrong. Maybe fear had no limits. Maybe a person had an inexhaustible supply waiting to rise up from a dark corner of the soul.

All she knew was that a new kind of terror now gripped her.

CHAPTER 15

Jake felt like an SOB.

With the help of Alfonso on the chestnut, he had rounded up the three runaway horses in the little canyon that drained the ambush valley. Now, after a two-hour delay, Nub, the *muchacho,* and the Cappses were strung out behind Jake as his Appaloosa traced six sets of hoofprints down a dusty course. The tracks seemed to go on and on, winding through rocky hills and navigating ravines, a spoor prone to disappearing abruptly with the lay of the land, only to reemerge as quickly and vanish again. It was a country loath to give up its secrets, but routing the bandits in the valley had given Jake reason for optimism.

If only he didn't feel the way he did.

Jake supposed that Annie would be as disappointed in him as he was in himself. When it came to the do's and don'ts of personal interactions, Annie had long been

Jake's compass. With Nub in particular, she had given him warning, and he had let something that had happened forty-seven years ago get the better of him.

The horses were tiring, reason enough to dismount and walk the animals. For a couple of miles, Jake trudged alone on point, leading his Appaloosa, but he finally summoned the courage to drop back abreast of Nub, who had his sorrel in tow well ahead of the others. The two of them hadn't spoken since their confrontation, and the foreman, now at Jake's left, clearly wanted to keep it that way, for he had the profile of a Buffalo nickel Indian as he kept his focus straight ahead.

"Want to tell you somethin'," Jake said quietly.

Dust, and more, clogged his throat as he focused on the upside-down *U*'s marking the trail ahead. For a while, he and Nub walked in silence, shoulder to shoulder but neither looking at the other.

"They was a boy, just sixteen," Jake continued. "Had a sister younger than him, that oak country in Mason County. He was there on the porch, and she was drawin' up water at the well, and Indians — he supposed they was Comanche — here they come a-shootin'. Devils was on them 'fore they

245

knowed it, and he runs in the house yellin'
to his mama and grabs up his Sharps. The
pneumonia taken his father the year before,
so he had the responsibility, you know,
takin' care of the family."

The background patter of hoofs was far
too gentle as Jake told it all: the mounted
demon seizing the sister, the mother plead-
ing outside the door, the rifle sights swinging across blue calico.

" 'Shoot her, shoot her!' " Jake recounted,
aware that Nub faced him now. " 'You got
to shoot!' — that's all the boy could hear.
That's all I can *still* hear, all this time later."

Jake began to blink a lot, and he turned
away with a quiet "Damn," not wanting the
younger man to see.

"Good Lord," said Nub. "Did . . . ?"

"I let them take her off." Jake's voice
didn't want to work. "My own sister, I let
them take her off. Found her next day
across the San Saba, clothes tore off and
buzzards ever'where."

"Lord Almighty," said Nub.

"If I'd've did my part, I could've spared
her. I pull that trigger and she's dead all the
same, but not that way, not with what they
done to her."

Nub went as silent as Jake, and for a while
there were only hoofbeats, tolling off the

246

regrets of a man tortured from boyhood.

"Back at headquarters, when Mrs. Graves . . ." When Nub spoke, his words didn't come any easier than Jake's. "She alluded to a burden, but I had no conception."

"Fourteen was all she was. That's all my sister will ever be. Them last moments . . . What she went through . . . My fault. Ever' bit of it, damn me to hell."

Jake turned and they stared at one another, two men who had been at odds but only one of them having understood the reason.

"Now you know," said Jake. "Liftin' a rifle against my own flesh — layin' blame on you for what happens next — seein' my sister dead ever' time I look at you 'cause you's Indian — now you know why."

It was time to remount. Taking a handful of the Appaloosa's mane, Jake twisted the stirrup into place and started to step up, only to hesitate and look back at Nub. Jake had danced around what had happened on the hogback, and now it was time to face it.

"No excuse," he said quietly. "Even if I'd heard right about Dru, never should've stuck a gun in your face. You deserve better."

Jake was man enough to know it, and man

enough to admit it. But the words he added were the most difficult to say. "Guess what I'm tellin' you is, I'm sorry."

He swung into the saddle and put distance between the two of them.

Buried in thought, he wasn't aware that Nub was set on overtaking him until the younger rider came abreast on his left.

"I appreciate your apology, and even more so, your confiding in me," said Nub, his voice subdued. "Dru never mentioned any of this."

"Never told her. Hell of a thing to carry around. She don't need to know."

"My mentor on the Singing Waters once told me every man's a product of his past. He may try to rise above it, but it's always there."

"Yeah."

"He was fond of quoting what Milton wrote in *Paradise Lost.* 'Long is the way and hard, that out of Hell leads up to light.' "

Too long and hard a way, thought Jake.

"But, Mr. Graves, I believe there's a way out."

Waiting, Jake stared at him.

"If there's a hell," said Nub, "there's a Heaven. If there's a devil, there's a God."

"That's the second time you said somethin' like that."

"It's important to me. More so than ever the last three days when it was imperative I be lifted up."

Lifted up. It was odd that Nub should phrase it that way, and Jake remembered again his mother's plea to let a Higher Power set him soaring on eagle wings. But he had too much for which to forgive himself.

"Mr. Graves," Nub added, "twice you've faced an impossible decision. No matter your choice, it would have been wrong. I cannot imagine your turmoil, but none of the blame is yours. It's the fault of evil incarnate, first in Comanches and then in bandits."

Nub leaned toward the Appaloosa and seemed ready to initiate a handshake, only to hold the impulse in check in apparent deference to societal conventions. But what he couldn't do with a gesture, he did with words.

"Sir, I offer you my own apology, for judging you unfairly all this time."

Gigging his sorrel, Nub pushed ahead, leaving Jake pondering life and death and all the things between.

Jesús Rentería had heard the stories about *tlahuelpuchi* all his life.

A shape-shifting witch. A *brujo* who changes into a glowing animal and goes in search of human blood to keep him alive. Perhaps he becomes a dog or a domestic cat, a figure slinking through dusty streets of a local village. Or maybe he takes to the skies as a buzzard or crow and travels great distances. He may even be forced to transform into an insect in order to gain entry to a secured home. But no matter the form *tlahuelpuchi* has taken, he must always become a man again before draining a victim's blood from the neck.

Rentería could not remember ever becoming an animal.

Maybe he had been unaware. Maybe he had been all of those things — a coyote and a turkey, a flea and a tick, even *vibora,* the devil-eyed snake — and had never realized it. Blinded by his need, how could he have known?

Sometimes Rentería wondered if he was just a man, a sick, sick man, driven mad by his early obsession with *tlahuelpuchi.* All he knew for certain was that once a moon he must feed — or die.

Serving as a Carrancista officer, and later as *capitán* of *bandidos,* it had been easy to slip away by night and satisfy his want in secrecy. The revolution and the lawlessness it had spawned along the border had given cover for his deeds. A baby was best, but a *señorita* was almost as nourishing. In a trying time, the blood of a grown man might sustain him, but only if he followed up with something purer within a few short days.

Two of those had already passed since Rentería had strung up the merchant by his heels and, upon being left alone in Capote Store, had drawn a knife across the throat and placed a cup below. Now the need was upon him again, exacerbated by the stress of battle. If he could rest for many hours, he might stave off the urgency, but stopping in broad daylight was out of the question.

Like waves lapping the bank of the *río,* the symptoms came and went, draping him across the saddle horn for miles, only to pass as his black pressed on. With each reoccurrence, he was always weaker, his craving greater, and within another day he would have no choice but to satisfy his need any way he could. Under other circumstances, he would have separated from the march and sought out the nearest village across the *río,* but Rentería was on a mission. Somehow he had to appease the devil twin so she would release him, and his only hope lay in getting her to that little clearing where Consuela's blood had run.

Consuela.

Across all the years and victims, the taste of her blood still lingered as the sweetest. It had also been the bitterest, and the bitter and sweet of his memories waged war as he looked back from his trotting horse at Consuela-who-wasn't-Consuela on the big dun. Every artery in her neck seemed to stand out, bulging rivulets throbbing with the beat of her heart.

For agonizing minutes, Rentería had deliberated over whom to choose, the yellow-haired *señorita* or *La Diablesa,* but now he was sure. No matter which devil from *infierno* had assumed the form of Consuela, hers was the blood he wanted, hers and no one else's.

Obsessed almost beyond control, he managed to wrench his gaze away and stare over his horse's head. The trail ahead rose and fell with the animal's gait, but all he could see was the bounce of those raven tresses against a neck drawing him like iron to a lodestone.

Dusk came creeping, an eerie, troubling dusk that hinted of unholy things waiting to prowl the night.

Rentería could ride no farther. Another weak spell had all but crippled him, and for the last mile he had barely clung to the black. Even as his desire for the devil twin grew, he longed as much for the hours of rest that might also restore his strength. Still, with an enemy pursuing, even the coming night would leave him vulnerable if he stopped.

That is, if Rentería were only a man. As an agent of evil, or so he believed, he could call on *la magia negra,* the black arts, just as he had done in *la cueva del diablo,* the devil's cave.

Pulling rein at a nook in an agave-dotted hill on the left, he instructed his men to prepare for camp. As they took charge of the captives, he slid off his mount and collapsed at the hoofs. Dragging himself up by means of the stirrup leather, he stumbled back up the trail, weaving through the horses until all that lay ahead were skulking shadows.

Rentería drew his bone-handled knife and sank to his knees. With the blood-caked blade, he scraped a clear spot in the horse tracks and set about carving strange figures in the dirt. Just ahead of a troubling dark falling quickly, the images took shape — a staff twisted with snakes, a bat-winged thing with the horns of a goat, a man or a wolf or something both less and more than either.

His handiwork finished, Rentería rocked back and forth over the sketches and murmured incantations in a language that he could voice but not understand. He supposed they were *el diablo's* words that flowed from his lips, for if a man could speak with the tongues of angels, he might also speak with the tongues of devils.

Whatever the words, Rentería cast them to the shadows that lay back up-trail.

CHAPTER 16

Astride his Appaloosa, Jake led the way through a hard dark that seemed alive.

Ever since nightfall, wolves had howled in the distance. From closer had come the *yip-yip* of coyotes, and twice Jake had heard the startling scream of a panther. Now, in his exhaustion, strange shadows seemed to float through the night, things that were both more and less than animals, wicked things that should have been reserved for his night-mares.

Maybe that's all they were — dream figures darting in and out of the here and now. No matter their true nature, Jake felt damned anxious, and the tension in his horse's back didn't ease his mind any.

"Eyes is playin' tricks on me," Bill Ike grumbled from behind.

"You see *fastasmas,* ghosts?" asked Alfonzo.

Bill Ike laughed derisively. "You Mexes

and your damned superstitions. I say anything about boogers?"

"I see something too, Bill Ike!" spoke up Bo.

"Hell, boy, much as you keep your nose stuck over a bottle, no wonder you's seein' things."

"Look yonder! Back over there!" said Bo. "There's things all around!"

Jake saw plenty, enough to raise the hair on the back of his neck, but he wasn't going to admit it. Varmints and bats always came out at night, he told himself.

"It *tlahuelpuchi*!" exclaimed Alfonso. "He bring the *fantasmas* and *nahuales*!"

"*Nahuales*, Alfonzo?" asked Nub.

"*Sí*, ghost animals that suck the blood. *Nahuales muy poderóso*, very strong."

Without warning, a revolver roared, and roared again, spooking Jake's horse.

"Lord Almighty!"

"What the hell!"

Jake didn't know who had yelled, and two more blasts rattled his eardrums as he drew rein and wheeled the Appaloosa.

"Get them off of me, Bill Ike!" cried Bo, fire flashing twice more from his Colt. "Bill Ike, get them off!"

"I-god, put that gun away!" said the older Capps. "Horse near throwed me!"

"Settle that boy down!" said Jake. "Anybody wonderin' where we's at knows it now. Settle the clabberhead down!"

"Don't like you callin' my boy names, Graves," growled Bill Ike.

"Think I give a damn what you like?"

"My boy's as white as you. Me too. We ain't wetbacks for you to play straw boss over."

Greedy damned devil's what you are, Jake wanted to tell him. Nevertheless, he had stayed quiet even after learning that Bill Ike had abandoned him in the earthquake, and for the sake of the same fragile unity between them, he held his tongue again. But that didn't keep Jake from admonishing Bo directly.

"You go shootin' anymore and they'll be boarcat hell to pay!"

"The things are everywhere!" contended Bo.

"Nothin' in the dark that ain't in the day."

But Alfonso remained unconvinced. "*Tlahuelpuchi* do this! He call on *el diablo*!"

"Ain't there anything we can do?" asked Bo.

"Bullets no *buenos* against *nahuales*!" said the *muchacho*.

"There's nothing?" pressed Bo.

"*Nahuales* no like the fire!"

Alfonzo's persistent talk led Jake to see even more things that weren't there — or were they? But whether they were real or imagined, panic had spread like wildfire, and he didn't know how to quell it. Fortunately, Nub spoke up with the voice of reason.

"We must compose ourselves. Alfonso, please refrain from exacerbating matters."

"¿Qué, Señor Nub?"

"He means quit your damned jabberin'," simplified Bill Ike. "I-god, you Mexes."

Nub's silhouette turned to Jake. "Mr. Graves, we're all exhausted and prone to suggestion. Rest and a fire would do wonders for our perception of things."

Maybe Nub believed Alfonso's wild talk about *nahaules.* Maybe this was his way of arguing the case for a protecting fire without causing greater alarm. Regardless, Jake had already been spooked enough by the flitting shadows, and he reined his horse about, checking left and right by starlight.

"Up in them Spanish daggers," he said, pointing. "Let's climb off and get that fire a-goin'."

Nub replayed everything he had learned over the past three days about Dru's father. The older man sat across a snapping fire from Nub, the firelight flickering in his weathered face and throwing his shadow across a giant yucca at his back. The deep scoring at Jake's temples affirmed the weariness in the gray eyes. They showed every mile, and more, of the brutal ride from the Cross C's, and in their exhaustion they seemed to open up a window into a part of him that Nub had never seen before. For all his gruffness, Jake now displayed the wounds of a man haunted since boyhood and still in search of redemption.

Or maybe the vulnerability had always been there, and it had been Nub's perception that had changed.

"Guess you got a bone to pick with me, Graves, way I spouted off at you," said Bill Ike. He sat to the right of Jake, the smoke spiraling up between the two.

Nub wondered where this was headed; Bill Ike wasn't the type to make amends.

"Shouldn't oughta got on the peck the way I done," Bill Ike continued. "We get back, I'd still like you to put in a good word with that girl's folks."

For all of Jake's response, he might as well have been back at the Cross C's. Unexpectedly, it was Bo who reacted from where he sat on the opposite side of Jake. Between sips from a bottle, he mumbled drunkenly to himself.

"Somethin' you want to say, boy?" asked Bill Ike. "Ain't seein' boogers no more, are you?"

Beyond the range of the firelight, the night rose up like a black and mysterious wall, but now it seemed no more threatening than any other night. Still, Bo cast a nervous glance over his shoulder.

"Need to start layin' that bottle down," Bill Ike continued. "Start showin' Graves you's the kind of man he can brag on to that little girl's folks."

Bo snorted. "You ain't got no say, him neither, 'bout me drinking."

His words were slurred and his tone disrespectful, whether from liquor or stress or the pain of his burns and the beating he had suffered in the storm. In obvious spite, he lifted the bottle again, the firelight painting his bruised face.

"I-god, boy," said Bill Ike, "you got a lot at stake here, Graves bein' who he is."

"Don't need him."

"Careful, boy," interrupted Bill Ike. "Gettin' them Cross C folks to have you, you's goin' to need him, all right, her own uncle."

Nub grew alarmed by where this was headed, but the words came so fast that he didn't know how to stop it.

"Don't need *him,* don't need *you,* don't need *any* of you old bastards," said Bo. "I get Ruthie back, I'll be sitting pretty, parents or no parents. We'll talk to them and get a preacher man or run off and find one, but one way or the other we's getting it done and they ain't got a choice but to have me, the baby coming and all."

For a moment, there was stony silence, the popping of wood tolling off the seconds. It was an ominous silence that threatened to explode the longer it persisted. Then the fire flared, and Nub watched through the leaping flames as Jake slipped his hand inside his coat to the bulge that awaited a cross-body draw. Stricken with fear, Nub expected him to pull out his .45 immediately, but the older man kept his hand hidden under the woolen garment as he turned to Bo.

"What are you sayin'?" Jake's words were quiet and carefully weighed, and in their considered delivery they carried more threat than if he had shouted.

"Huh?" asked Bo, facing him.

"What the hell you sayin'?" This time, Jake's voice trembled with barely contained rage.

For a moment more, Bo seemed clueless, his brow ridged, his head tilting to the side, and then all at once he blanched and his jaw fell. Recoiling, he turned and began scrambling away, his boots kicking over the fire ring rocks and throwing sparks into the night. But maybe the devil in the dark was more frightening than the devil at the fire, for without ever gaining his feet, he whirled back to Ruthie's uncle.

"For God's sake, Graves!" he cried, throwing his hands out defensively.

Jake was on his feet now, a terrible picture of judgment advancing one slow step at a time, his hand ready inside his coat, the flames shining in his eyes like the fires of perdition.

Nub rose in fear. "Mr. Graves . . ."

But Jake wouldn't be distracted. Coming to a stop at Bo's ash-covered boots, he hovered over the cowering man who had let slip a dangerous secret a second time.

"Leave my boy be, Graves."

With a glance, Nub found Bill Ike standing over the blaze, a Bisley Model Colt down along his thigh capturing firelight.

"Graves," repeated Bill Ike, "leave my boy be."

But Jake held his position, his forearm frozen across his chest, his hand still hidden in his coat.

"Good Lord, Mr. Graves," implored Nub,

trying to project calm. "Remember Dru, remember Miss Ruthie."

"I-god, better listen to him," warned Bill Ike. "Shoot my boy and you ain't ridin' out of here."

Interrupted, Nub continued to plead with Jake.

"You're Dru's father, Miss Ruthie's uncle. Were you to shoot Bo, and you and Mr. Capps shoot one another, to what fate are you consigning the girls?"

For the first time, Jake looked at him.

Nub went on. "Mr. Graves, I was wrong when I questioned your character. You're too good a man to deny Miss Ruthie's child a father. You're too good a man to let emotion and impulse rob Dru and Miss Ruthie of their only hope."

Nub had one card left to play, and he used it.

"Mr. Graves, I cannot do this alone."

For a long while, the firelight danced in Jake's face as the two of them stared at one another. Then the older man withdrew his empty hand from his coat and looked down at Bo again.

"Guess her father gets first shot, anyhow," said Jake. "If he was to miss . . ."

Turning, he started away from Bo, and as Nub watched the older man's every step, he found more and more reason to breathe easier. Now the fire merely crackled, adding to the peace, and then a panther's far-off scream presaged the sudden snap of a revolver hammer against a spent cartridge — a sound nearly as piercing as a gunshot.

Nub spun, hearing it snap a second time, and saw the fire gleaming in the pearl grip of Bo's .41 Colt.

Lord Almighty!

Lying on his hip, Bo trained his revolver in Jake's general direction, although from Nub's perspective it was impossible to determine his exact target. There were voices in the night — one may have been Nub's — and more revolvers that flashed firelight, and abruptly Jake had swung about, his shadow falling across the sprawled man, his .45 New Service six-shooter cocked and ready.

"You try shootin' me?" growled Jake. "You damned coward, you try shootin' me in the back?"

"God, no, Graves!" exclaimed Bo, lowering his revolver. "The shadows was back! They was all around like before!"

Nub took a quick look. All he saw were sparks trailing off into a night no different than a thousand others.

"You heard my boy, Graves."

A second revolver hammer clicked back, and when Nub turned to Bill Ike, he found a full-fledged Mexican standoff in progress. With a shaky, extended arm, Bill Ike had taken aim at Jake, who seemed determined to strike as much fear as possible into Bo by the threat of his .45. The restraint of two index fingers dictated life or death for so many, and Nub searched for the right words to say.

"Sirs, I remind you of our greater goal," he said calmly.

For tense seconds, the unwinnable confrontation persisted, the very future hanging in the balance. Then Jake relaxed his gun arm, inducing Bill Ike to do the same, and it was over.

Maybe Bo had intended to shoot shadows that were more than shadows, and maybe he hadn't. As the night and its mysteries brought all of them back to the fire, Nub was just glad the worthless drunk had forgotten to reload after emptying his .41 from the stirrups of his roan.

"Gotta hand it to you, boy, gettin' that little girl bred the way you done. Fixed it so you's got the whole Cross C's."

Lying in his bedroll beside the fire ring, Nub heard Bill Ike talking with Bo in hushed tones from across the hissing flames. Their conversation had awakened him moments ago, and at first he had wished that they would join Jake and Alfonso in quiet sleep. Now, though, Nub opened his eyes to the flames tossing through a notch in the upright rocks and listened.

"I-god, feathered your nest good, didn't you?" Bill Ike continued. "Mine too, I guess."

Staring into the muzzle of Jake's .45 had sobered Bo considerably. "It's always 'Bill Ike this, Bill Ike that,' " said Bo. "Me all burned and beat up, get a gun shoved in my face, and everything's still about Bill Ike."

"Ain't true, boy. Can't a ol' daddy be proud you's worked it so we's both in the money?"

Bo breathed sharply. "Never crossed your mind, did it, that I might really care about her. Ruthie's the only good thing ever happened to me, growing up around a SOB like you."

"That's no way to talk, all the things I done for you. Coulda turned you and your mama out in the cold, she whorin' around the way she was. She's the one finally run off and left you. I reckon it's still got to smart, you just six-year-old."

"You chased her off. You beat her and

chased her off. Soon's she wasn't around anymore to take things out on, you started in on me."

"Let's forget all that, boy," urged Bill Ike. "You's fixin' to be up in high cotton, and I know you ain't goin' to forget your ol' daddy."

"My old daddy," Bo repeatedly sarcastically. "It's just as well it ain't you, Bill Ike. 'Cause with it bein' somebody else, maybe there's still a chance for me, the way Ruthie says there is."

"Wish you wouldn't keep bringin' that up."

"It's all I got to hope on. I don't want nothing to do with you anymore. Bad enough you raised me, the way you turned me to drink. I ever get away, be with Ruthie, maybe I won't turn out like you."

The voices died away, and there was only the sputtering of the fire and the far-off howl of a wolf. But Nub was wide awake now, weighing everything he had thought about Bo in light of a six-year-old abandoned to the cruelties of a profligate like Bill Ike Capps.

CHAPTER 17

Hours of sleep had restored Jesús Rentería's strength, but as he rode under a sunrise sky, he knew he must feed today or die.

Two things did he regret above all others in his thirty-six years. Chief among them had been the heinous deed he had perpetrated against Consuela. And second had been the disquiet he had generated in their younger brother Roberto, whose knowing glare had driven him from their home.

Consuela, Rentería could never atone for, except for whatever penance her devil twin would demand at the place where the blood had run. But Roberto was another matter, and his young face, ashen and convicting in the truth about Consuela's death, had stayed with Rentería across all the years. Rentería had longed to erase that memory of a child he had cruelly stripped of trust and innocence, but there had never seemed a way.

Until now.

From the moment Rentería had yielded to the summons from the home of his youth, he had known he would pass through the village of Los Fresnos, the upstream gateway to the Rio Grande fields where *el diablo* had stolen away his soul. In Rentería's Carrancista command had been a onetime resident of Los Fresnos, and from him Rentería had found out that Roberto worked in the vicinity of the small village as a *candelillero,* or wax maker. Roberto and Rentería had learned the trade from their father, who prior to his disability had harvested candelilla from the desert and extracted its wax. The plant, consisting of tightly bunched, gray-green stalks growing one or two feet high, offered financial return in a remote region where subsistence farming dominated.

On the outskirts of the adobe village shining in the sunburst of a new day, Rentería rode upon a black cur hobbling on three legs down the dusty street. The animal, so sickly with mange that its rib cage showed, slung its head around and bared its teeth, a low growl rising up from its throat. But there must have been something about Rentería, riding ahead of the others, that took all the fight out of the cur. As soon as Rentería came abreast, the animal yelped and retreated into the shadows between white-plastered walls.

There, backed against a pole fence, the mongrel turned and kept up its pitiful shriek, as though it perceived things about Rentería that a man could not.

A curse on his lips, Rentería drew rein and came up with his .45 automatic. With a quick bullet, he would put an end to the yelping, but as he took aim, he couldn't bring himself to shoot.

Whether a cur dog announced it to the world, or was silenced by a gunshot, Rentería knew he would remain what he was: a thing damned, with no hope for escape but death.

His spirits sinking, threatening to sap the fragile strength he had regained, Rentería rode on. At a tin lean-to against a sunlit mud wall, he came upon a Mexican man with a withered arm squatting at a fire and cooking tortillas on a crude griddle.

"*¿Dónde encontraré a* Roberto Rentería?" Rentería asked.

"The *candelillero, sí,*" said the man, rising. Pointing into the bright east horizon, he provided directions to Roberto's camp with a few words and an abundance of hand gestures.

Bearing left as instructed, Rentería led the other riders into a sun burning low in the sky. As they navigated a narrow burro trail through ocotillo and lechuguilla, two of his men addressed him, one after the other.

"Where are we going, *Capitán*?"

"*Por favor,* where are you taking us?"

When they had posed the same questions two days before, Rentería had answered, "To the ends of purgatory." Now, as he remained silent, he wondered if he had bypassed that place of temporary punishment. Was the fiery wheel ahead really the sun, or had *el diablo* opened a gateway to hell just for him?

Whatever its nature, Rentería rode toward it a full hour before a plume of smoke rose up out of the distant yucca and drifted across its face. Smoke was a sure sign of an active wax camp, and another few minutes brought him near the small operation on an elevated flat near a bend of the Rio Grande.

Up through the creosote bushes on Rentería's right came a *muchacho,* leading a burro laden on each side with barrels sloshing water acquired at the river. No more than twelve, the boy bore a startling resemblance to Roberto as he remembered him: a slender, black-haired youth with a distinctive way of biting his lip and cocking his head toward his left shoulder. The *mucha-cho* also had the same large eyes of someone always inquisitive, a trait that must have led Roberto to follow Rentería on the day the blood had run.

Watching the boy approach with the burro on this morning in 1917, it was easy for Rentería to imagine that this was his brother, unchanged across all the years. A part of Rentería wanted to take the *mucha-cho* in his arms and pretend that he, too, was a youth again, and that the day of his dark awakening had never come. Rentería had never wept since the moment he had drawn Consuela's lifeless body to his breast and wet her hair with his cheeks, but now the emotion stung his eyes.

If he could only go back and relive the time of innocence . . . If only . . . If only . . .

All at once, the *muchacho's* blurry form was alongside, holding the burro.

"*¿Como se llama?*" Rentería asked. A knot hung in his throat.

"Luis Rentería." Even the boy's voice was much like the young Roberto's.

Rentería checked the camp. Fifty yards ahead, where gray smoke churned up from a large pit fire, the support posts of a brush shelter framed a hunched laborer wearing a sombrero.

"*¿Es este tu padre?*" asked Rentería. "That your father?"

"*Sí.*"

Shaded, the *candelillero* had his back turned as he worked, but Rentería understood what he was doing. A large, steel vat was in place, suspended over the coals, and as the candelilla boiled in acidic water, a waxy foam floated to the top. With an *espumador,* or perforated skimmer, the man transferred the foam into a mold bucket for separation, cooling, and hardening. Eventually, the raw wax would be broken into chunks and placed in burlap bags.

To the left of the brush shelter was a high stack of harvested candelilla ready for extraction, as well as a large store of creosote brush for stoking the fire. Back away from the piles, far enough so that drifting smoke wouldn't be a problem, lay a primitive A-frame hut. Thatched with dried candelilla, the shelter's entry was protected from the elements by a hanging woolen blanket. Even farther away stirred several hobbled burros, waiting to haul the bagged wax to a buyer.

Roberto clearly lived a hard life, but Rentería would have traded his own accursed existence for his brother's in an instant.

Ordering that only the devil twin accompany him, Rentería motioned for the *muchacho* to lead the way. With the plodding burro setting the pace, Rentería rode farther into the past — a full twenty years by the time he pulled rein a few yards shy of the man.

"*Papá, hombres* are here," informed the boy.

The *candelillero* glanced over his shoulder, and then laid aside the skimmer and rose to wipe his hands on his ragged cotton trousers. His leather shoes were pitiful, eaten away from stamping candelilla down to the level of the vat's corrosive water. When the man turned, Rentería recognized his young brother in a sun-browned face that, even at age thirty-two, was already lined at the eyes and gray-stubbled. But Roberto seemed not to know him, for the *candelillero* only peered up at Rentería curiously before bending his head to the side so he could see the riders behind.

Rentería looked back too, and asked the devil twin to dismount. After both of them had stepped down and secured their horses to a creosote bush, he escorted her up before Roberto.

For a long time, the two men studied one another, the emotion stealing away the words Rentería wanted to say. Here was his sole connection with the days of his youth. They seemed so long ago, and yet so near, those days when both of them had been so naïve. Even for peons, the world had offered promise and hope. Then had come *tlahuelpuchi,* first as a mere obsession, and finally as the dark shadow that would rule Rentería's every breath.

For a few seconds more, Rentería relived so many things, and then a baby's cry drew his attention to the hut. In an instant, a great thirst rose up inside him. Thatch walls and the hanging blanket hid what was inside, but nothing could mute the wails. *Ay Dios,* in the place where he had once had a soul, a fever began to burn, a consuming fire that only one thing could extinguish.

"What do you want, *señor?*"

Roberto's question in Spanish seemed to come from a great distance, so lost in obsession was Rentería. He looked back at his brother, but the crying drew his gaze again to the thatch walls.

"*Señor,*" Roberto repeated. "What do you want?"

With the wails abruptly subsiding, Roberto's words must have carried to the hut, for the hanging blanket rippled and a sickly *señora* with questioning eyes stepped out with a nursing baby at her breast.

For a third time, Roberto spoke. *"Señor?"*

With willpower he didn't think he had, Rentería tore his eyes away from mother and child, but the image of an infant's throbbing arteries stayed with him.

"Roberto, *mi hermano,*" Rentería said quietly. "It's me, Jesús, your brother."

For a few seconds, Roberto just stared — and then his face went deathly white.

"¡Madre de Dios!" he cried, recoiling. "Go away! Child of *el diablo,* go away!"

Rentería stretched out an imploring arm. "It's all right, my brother. I've brought Consuela back. See our sister? Look how she's grown!"

Even as Roberto looked, his wide eyes showed only dread.

"What do you mean? Consuela's dead! I saw you kill her and then — go away, *tlahuelpuchi*!"

Confused, Rentería glanced at the woman beside him. "It's Consuela, Roberto — can't you see? I've brought her back. I take her to the place where the blood ran."

But Roberto couldn't see.

"Tlahuelpuchi!" he said again, retreating more. "Go back to *infierno*!"

"It's not my fault, *mi hermano. Lo siento,* I'm not to blame."

Now there was more than revulsion in Roberto's features; his face became a mask of rage.

"It *is* your fault, Jesús!" he charged. "From your first Holy Communion, your fault!"

"My first . . . ?"

"You knocked the chalice away! You told the *padre* you were the seed of *el diablo.* Twelve and you chose *el diablo* over Jesucristo!"

Rentería didn't want to remember. He preferred to believe that he had been as much a victim as Consuela and all the others who had felt his knife at their throats over the years.

"You lie!" he said. "It's not my fault. You lie!"

"How could you be this way, Jesús?" pressed his brother. "Mama and Papa, they gave you Jesucristo's name — how could you kill our sister?"

The memory was too vivid, the pain of it too great, made all the more so because it had been dredged up out of hell by someone whose forgiveness Rentería needed. But Roberto wasn't through.

"*Fuera de aquí!* Go away and die, *tlahuel-puchi*! By your own hand — die!"

Rentería could endure no more. Lunging, he seized his brother by the throat with a vise of a hand.

"*Sí,* I'm *tlahuelpuchi*! Maybe I come back tonight and kill your baby *chupado por el brujo,* sucked by the witch!"

Shoving him back, Rentería left his brother bent over and struggling for air and mounted up with Consuela-who-wasn't-Consuela. But as he turned his black down-river, a powerful word also went with him, vexing and dominating.

Die.

Roberto and the *tezlitac* — the two people in the world who recognized him for what he was — had told him the same thing, and maybe there was no better place for it than the little clearing where the blood had run.

CHAPTER 18

"Tell me again, *Señor* Jake. How I not let Rentería lead Alfonso this way, that, even after *tlahuelpuchi* dead."

They rode into the morning sun, the *muchacho* on Jake's left and the others strung out behind in the creosote. Not long after sunup, they had passed through a small village, where a man with a withered arm had told them of four *hombres* and two white *señoritas* and pointed to the bright east sky. Now, half an hour later, Jake and the *muchacho* bore toward a distant column of smoke.

"How I do it, get away from him?" Alfonso added.

Checking, Jake confirmed in the *muchacho's* slumped shoulders that he was as dispirited as his voice suggested.

"Memories eatin' you up awful bad, ain't they," said Jake.

"It like it just happen, my sister, *mi mamá,*

mi papá. Like they die all over again."

Jake knew what he meant. Ever since Rentería and his men had carried Dru and Ruthie away, it was as if he relived every moment of the terrible search for his own sister.

"Help me, *Señor* Jake," pressed Alfonso. "I sleep, *fantasmas* there. I wake, *fantasmas* there. *Fantasmas* there all time."

Fantasmas. The ghosts of things past, thought Jake, always present, always haunting. Would they ever go away, for either of them?

"Somebody, they tell you what to do when you still *muchacho,*" reminded Alfonso. "*Por favor,* say to me again."

More and more, Jake had dwelled on his mother's long-ago plea. He could still see her wan face glowing in the soft lamplight, still smell the kerosene as the wick burned with a quiet purr. He could see a candle bug circle the smutty globe, testing the warmth that he could feel from where he sat around the corner of the table from this frail woman who had lost much and yet clung to faith. But most of all, Jake could see the leather-bound book between them, its thin pages, with notes scribbled in the margins, open to the passage she had repeated ever since he had dropped to his knees before her and wept his regret.

Humble yourselves in the sight of the Lord, and he shall lift you up.

Maybe Jake could still allow it to happen. Maybe it wasn't too late, even after forty-seven years.

Maybe, just maybe. In a search for peace, even acknowledging a *maybe* was a step he had never taken before.

He must have spoken aloud, considering what Alfonso said.

"I want Jesucristo lift me up like she say, *Señor* Jake." The *muchacho* looked skyward, and as he crossed himself, a fervent appeal broke from his lips. *"¡Mi Padre, mi Padre, por favor, mi Padre!"*

Then Alfonso faced Jake again, and his hand moved to the bone handle of his sheathed machete.

"Sí," he said, setting his young jaw in fierce determination, "I want Jesucristo lift me up. But first *tlahuelpuchi* die."

They rode on, the rising smoke nearing, and soon met a burro train that gave all indications of having been hastily thrown together. The loads were disorderly, with loose items rattling and blankets dragging the ground. Packing a burro was an art that people along the border had mastered, but this train looked as if time had been more

281

important than efficiency.

On point, a *muchacho* tugged on a tow rope to urge the lead burro to greater speed, while a few animals behind, a sickly *señora* with a small baby trudged through the boiling dust. Well behind her, a Mexican man hurried the drags along by the force of frequent lashes with a section of river cane.

Neither the *muchacho* nor *señora* looked up as they brushed past on Jake's left with the stronger burros. But as the sombreroed man approached with the drags, Jake took his Appaloosa across their path and forced him to stop.

"Four men, two girls a-horseback," said Jake. "You seen them?"

The Mexican eyed him suspiciously before shouting ahead to the *muchacho*. "*¡Vaya con prisa!* Hurry, Luis!"

"Asked you a question," said Jake.

The Mexican checked the riders behind Jake as the burro train squeezed past their horses. "You with Jesús Rentería?" the man asked in halting English.

"No," said Jake. "You got somethin' to do with him?"

"No, *señor*. He *mi hermano,* my brother, but we leave this place *con prisa.*"

"How come?"

"He come back tonight to kill *niño, chu-*

pado por el brujo."

There was that phrase yet again, *sucked by the witch.*

"He's your brother?" repeated Jake.

"*Sí,* he a *tlahuelpuchi* since we *muchachos.* He come my camp, first time *veinte* years."

"Them girls — how they look?"

"*Muy* afraid. They have reason."

"What you mean, reason?"

"They something to you, *señor?*"

"My daughter and niece," said Jake. "They carried them off three days ago. Been chasin' after them all this time."

"Then you must hurry, *señor.* Jesús have the blood fever in his eyes. Maybe he not wait for night and come for my *niño.* Maybe he take the *señoritas'* blood before sun go down."

Good God.

Jake lifted his gaze past the Mexican and quickly searched the distance through the stirring dust. "How long since you seen them?"

"*Treinta minutos.*"

"Half hour's all?"

"Not so many, maybe."

"Burros tromped out the tracks — which way they headed?"

"Where we *muchachos.* To place he kill our sister Consuela and drink the blood."

"He done *what*?"

"*Sí,* it is so. Now he think dark-hair *se-ñorita* Consuela. Maybe he drink her blood same place."

"Good Lord!" exclaimed Nub from be-hind Jake. "Direct us to it!"

"It by *descanso* on a, how you say? Bluff? *Sí,* bluff. I put *descanso* there *muchos* years, give Consuela peace."

Descanso. From Jake's decades on the border, he was familiar with the practice. When pallbearers of Mexican heritage car-ried a coffin to a graveyard, the distance might force a rest stop, or *descanso,* at which point a cross would be erected as a memorial.

"We must make haste, Mr. Graves!" urged Nub.

Jake knew it, and he pressed the Mexican. "How we get there? Hurry up and tell me!"

With gestures and fast words, the man told Jake what he wanted to know.

"One thing more, *señor,*" Rentería's brother added. "Kill him! Kill him for *mi fa-milia, mi niño!*"

"I chop the head!" spoke up Alfonso.

When Jake glanced back, he saw the machete blade flashing in the sunlight.

"*Sí, la cabeza,* the head!" said the man. "*Tlahuelpuchi* no die unless by own hand or somebody cut the head! *Vaya con Dios!*"

A moment later, Jake had touched spurs to his horse's rib cage and was away through the slapping creosote, a desperate man in a desperate race that had been brewing for forty-seven years.

"We must overtake them in time, Mr. Graves. I . . . I don't know how I could face life without Dru."

Jake had his horse in a lope abreast of Nub and his white-lathered sorrel on the left. The pace through devil cholla and dragon's blood was demanding on animals that had lost so much flesh, and between his thighs Jake could feel the Appaloosa struggle. Nub's mount was no less wearied, its stride ragged, its breathing labored. But both horses seemed willing to give their all, to run to their deaths if necessary — the kind of grit that separated cow horses from nags, and men of courage from the timid.

Nub was a man of courage.

Jake had recognized it ever since the attack at headquarters, but even to himself, he had refused to acknowledge so worthy a trait in an Indian set on marrying his daughter. Nevertheless, for three days he had weighed Nub's character against that of Bo and Bill Ike and, for that matter, every man with whom he had ridden in the Rangers and mounted inspectors. Was there any of them Jake would rather have had beside him right now? What did that say about his reluctance to accept the notion of Dru in Nub's arms?

Jake didn't know, but he realized that it said more about himself than it did about Nub.

"I suppose my girl thinks a lot of you," Jake said over the drum of hoofs.

"Yes, sir. She says the Lord brought us together. I believe His hand is upon our lives."

"You think He cares that much?"

"Yes, sir, I do."

"The whole world's out there. All them people. The sky and the moon. Stars up there at night. How come He'd care about the two of you?"

"He does, Mr. Graves. That's all I can say."

For a few seconds, Jake rode in silence, dwelling on so many things. "Then how come Him to let my sister get killed? Dru and Ruthie get carried off?"

"Sir, I don't pretend to have the answers. Why bad things happen to good people is something I cannot begin to fathom. But I *will* tell you this: We have His promise that all things work together for good for those of us who love Him. Perhaps not in our lifetimes, but ultimately. What the world intends for evil, the Lord uses for good."

Again, Jake listened to the rhythmic hoofs for several strides of his Appaloosa. "You and my mama would've got along good. Guess that says somethin' about you."

When he looked at Nub, Jake thought he read surprise in his face. Still, Jake didn't expect the response he received.

"Dru's character speaks well of *you,* Mr. Graves. I hope you realize that the influence of you and Mrs. Graves on her life has made her the exceptional person she is."

Pondering, Jake looked down at his saddle horn. "Never was around as much as I'd liked to been," he confessed. "Her mama done most of the raisin'."

"Nevertheless, you have had an impact, and for that I'm appreciative."

They pushed through the abandoned wax camp and picked up horse tracks across a rugged tableland well above the river, and with every passing agave and prickly pear stand, the trail looked fresher. They were riding Rentería down, one lunging stride at a time, but if what his brother had said was true, it might not be fast enough. Maybe Rentería wasn't a monster, as the brother and old woman and Alfonso had claimed;

that kind of talk was so foreign to Jake's experiences that he didn't know what to make of it. But there was no doubt that a deranged man could kill just as surely.

Twisting around in the saddle, Jake found the Cappses close behind.

"We's goin' up against 'em!" he shouted. "They'll be loaded for bear, so's we got to be ready!"

Straightening, Jake searched the distance for dust or the glint of a firearm, but a range of rocky hills ahead hid too much. All he could do was hope that everyone heeded his warning.

"Better get your six-shooter loaded, boy."

From behind, Bill Ike's gruff voice was distinct over the hoofbeats, but there was no reply.

"Said, dig out your .41 shells," Bill Ike reiterated. "Better listen to your ol' —"

"Quit telling me what to do," Bo interrupted. "Gun can't hold but so many."

"So you done —"

"Never learned much from you, 'cept being mean. But I'm pretty sure I can count to six."

"Just worried 'bout you, boy. That's all."

"Huh! Only person you ever worry about's Bill Ike."

"Ain't true," said Bill Ike. "Ain't true at

all. I'd give my sorry life for yours. No question 'bout it, son."

"*Son,*" Bo repeated with a caustic laugh. "Listen, you old devil. You beat the daylights out of me when I was little for calling you papa. I don't call you papa, and you don't call me son."

"I'm shootin' straight with you, boy, how much you mean to me. Yeah, maybe sounds like all I want's a cut of the Cross C's, but you's all I got. I lose you and I ain't got nothin'."

"Then you got nothing, Bill Ike, 'cause you and me's done. I get Ruthie back and we got our own lives here on out."

Except for the pound of hoofs against turf, there was an unsettling silence that affected even Jake. He had no use for Bill Ike Capps; hell, the man had trained a revolver on him just hours before. But as a father, Jake couldn't help but feel for him. After all, if things didn't go right, Jake, too, stood to lose the very person who made him a father, and he just couldn't imagine it.

When Bill Ike addressed Bo again, Jake heard in his voice the same tenderness that had surprised him on the morning after Bo had passed out in the fire.

"I know you's awful riled at me," said Bill Ike, "but 'member what I'm tellin' you. My life for yours, boy. Damned right — my life for yours."

Maybe only a fool would trust anything Bill Ike Capps had to say, but it was the same promise Jake had sworn to himself about Dru and Ruthie.

All the faces went with Rentería.

They were young faces mainly, the angelic features of innocent babies unaware that the promise of the future would never be theirs. Dependent, trusting, completely blind to evil, each of them had slept a terrible sleep of Rentería's design. Sometimes there had been *señoritas,* and occasionally men of years, such as the storekeeper, but in one and all, Rentería had perpetrated a long goodbye from which there was no return.

And merely so he could live.

Except in the case of his sister, regret had long since faded, replaced by callous disregard. Gone was any concern for denying life to the guiltless, or for bringing grief to family members. A mass murderer he had been, or he would not have been at all.

But now, strangely, Rentería seemed to shoulder the torment of every one of them — each *niño* and *señorita* and *hombre* whose lifeblood he had taken, each an-

290

guished mother who had held her dead baby to her breast, all the loved ones doomed to relive their respective losses on the way to graves of their own.

During Rentería's youth, the old *padre* had told him that Jesucristo had borne the sins of the world. Maybe now the guilt of the world had fallen on Rentería.

He saw the faces everywhere, the young who would never be old, the *señoritas* who would never be mothers, the men without blame who would die with mouths twisted in agony. They were in every rock and yucca, these haunting figures, in every agave and clump of bear grass. Ghosts from his past, always beckoning, they drew him up through dark boulders forged in fire and under daunting crags. Down a narrow gulch they led him, and out onto a boulder-strewn point on a long, windy rim that fell away suddenly at his horse's breast. The slope dropped in two stages, the first more than fifty feet through projecting rocks and clinging cacti to a house-sized flat with a large weathered cross of cottonwood, and the second stage a hundred feet more to the *río*'s brushy bottomland.

Two hundred yards down and away amid tall cane, screwbeans, mesquites, and saltbush, the winter-bared limbs of a black willow marked the west side of a small clearing. There, more vivid than ever, the faces gathered, one for every month of the past twenty years.

Sí, from the very place where Consuela's blood had run, they stared up at him, every one of Rentería's victims, and he had no choice but to surrender to their siren call.

Spellbound, he was unaware that one of his men had reconnoitered back up-trail, until the bandit pulled rein alongside and reported breathlessly.

"*Cinco hombres, Capitán!* Just minutes behind!"

Rentería looked past the Mexican's wide eyes at the range of hills through which they had passed, and then back at the bewitching faces near the *río.* Turning in the saddle, he traced the east-trending rim to a location forty yards away, where enormous, hewn boulders perched like *lechuzas,* shape-shifting witch owls. Leaning over his animal's shoulder, Rentería checked the sturdy cross on the tier below him, assessing angles and considering. Then once again the faces in the place stained by Consuela's blood seized his attention.

And he knew that he mustn't let anything keep the devil twin and him from a date twenty years in the making.

CHAPTER 19

Jake rode a trail as recent as this very hour and as old as 1870.

It was a trail of regret mainly, a gloomy trace that carried him across forty-seven years. It had begun down the sights of a Sharps on the porch of a homestead, and from there it had led to a forsaken grave on the San Saba, on past the Cross C headquarters, and now to these hovering crags where the echoes of his Appaloosa's hoofbeats seemed to mock his feeble hopes. Already, he was a defeated man, doomed to revisit his sister's body in the guise of Dru and Ruthie, and he had nothing to urge him on but his mother's plea to let someone he had shoved aside lift him up.

Three men and a *muchacho* may have ridden with Jake, but in many ways he was alone, bearing a load that seemed heavier than ever before. He could smell the honeysuckle from his sister's grave at springtime, a sickening stench that roiled his stomach even in the dead of a Chihuahuan Desert winter. They had buried her torn clothes with her, but from every ocotillo stalk they seemed to flap in the gusts, dark-stained flags flying in constant reminder. Worst was the wind's sough through this pass, for it seemed to cry out with the voices of his sister and Dru and Ruthie — three guiltless young women for whom he had failed to grant compassionate deaths.

Jake was in the lead as he and the other riders cautiously navigated a narrow gorge and spilled out onto a place just as Rentería's brother had described: the solid rock footing deep-toned under the hoofs, the sudden drop-off stretching east past thirteen huge boulders huddled like a coven of *brujos,* the open floodplain and riparian brush of the Rio Grande down and away from the rim. Taking the Appaloosa closer to the edge, he saw the upright cottonwood timber begin to appear from a hidden shelf below. From his perspective, it rose higher over the rim with his pony's advance, until the thick crossbar was visible.

The *descanso,* the brother had called the memorial, and it overlooked the sparkling river and, on the near side, a small clearing among tall cane and screwbeans, saltbush and mesquites, as well as a single black willow.

Under the rim, the rubbly slope angled down steeply through outcrops and pitaya, and as Jake drew rein, an intervening boulder still hid the cross's base. Abruptly, over the whistling wind, he heard a muffled moan from below.

Jake already had his carbine out, but now he slid his fingers inside the lever port, ready to throw a .44 Special round into the chamber.

"You hear that, sir?" Nub quickly whispered from nearby.

There were more whispers from behind, maybe from Bo, but Jake was already edging the Appaloosa along the rim. Another horse came abreast on his left as the full cross broke into view, and a frantic voice blurted what Jake saw for himself.

"Ruthie! They got her tied!" said Bo.

Facing the rimrock, Ruthie sat against the cross, her arms drawn back around the timber. A gag creased her mouth, and her blond hair tossed in the wind as she looked up in obvious recognition. Even from fifty or so feet above, Jake could see alarm in her features, and she began to groan and repeatedly tilt her head to her right shoulder.

Something was astir, and Jake knew it. He

levered a cartridge into the chamber and scouted with a law officer's eye: up the empty rim on one side and down it to the ganged boulders on the other, left and right across the slope under his horse's breast, behind to the looming crags and ahead to the sunken floodplain. The situation called for caution, but unexpectedly Bo was off his roan and scrambling over the rim.

"Hold it!" said Jake. "This ain't right!"

There was no stopping Bo; maybe there was something worthwhile in him after all. Jake, too, got caught up in the moment, letting emotion instead of sound judgment take control. God Almighty, that was his *niece* down there, she and her unborn baby, and where Ruthie was, Dru might be as well.

Dismounting with a shout for Alfonso to take his horse, Jake dropped off the rim and sat back against the rolling rubble. With both hands on his carbine, he let the downward pull carry him between bruising boulders and clawing cacti. A barely controlled slide, his descent was reckless, and just to the right of the lower tier it came to a jarring stop at a jumble of rocks that he fended off with his boots.

Sprawled on his back, he sat up quickly and scanned with his carbine. Over a low outcrop on his left, he found the small flat ringed by modest boulders on three sides and a jagged pitch of black rock above. The sunlight reflecting off the dark rocks created a soft, golden hue that seemed to rise up from the soil and bathe the cottonwood timbers — one upright, one across. The spring after the attack in Mason County, Jake had promised his mother that he would set a cross at his sister's grave, but upon reaching the blooming honeysuckle, he had only wept and ridden on, never to return home. Now, seeing this sign of his mother's faith loom over his niece thirty feet away, Jake added one more entry to his regrets.

"Ruthie! We's come for you!"

She turned at Jake's cry, but someone else shouted her name as well. Climbing to his feet, Jake saw Bo emerge from behind a boulder closer to Ruthie, and just as Bill Ike slid into view on his son's heels, the younger man bolted for the girl.

Jake, too, broke for her, but warily, checking for trouble over the barrel of his Marlin. The rocks and overhead pitch looked clear, but Ruthie shook her head frantically and her muffled groans took on a desperate note.

Bo reached her first and set to work on the gag, but Jake was more concerned with her bonds. He came up behind the cross, against which Ruthie's chafed wrists were tied over each other. From here, he could see the upright timber, Ruthie, and Bo almost in a line, while off at an angle to the left, Bill Ike and his Bisley revolver held a leery position behind a boulder.

But what Jake couldn't see were the shooters.

The gunfire erupted without warning, wood exploding from the post just above Jake's head. Even as he recoiled, Jake cursed himself for being lured into danger like a rat to a trap. He came up with his carbine and scanned the high rimrock, but saw nothing as dirt kicked up around Ruthie and more wood chips flew. With a cry Bo went down, clutching his leg, and Jake had no choice but to fall back, the bullets somehow missing him as he dived for the nearest cover.

He came down on his belly in a cleft between angular boulders barely higher than his shoulders, a dangerous position that left his legs exposed until he drew up his knees. Ruthie and the cross were directly behind him now, and through a small notch in the rocks that lined the drop-off at his face, he could see the open floodplain a hundred feet below and the brush line eighty yards beyond. Twisting around, he peered over the adjacent boulder and saw gun smoke drifting along the rim. Tracing it back, he located muzzle flashes and stirring horses between the great, black boulders that Rentería's brother had compared to witches.

"Help me, Bill Ike! You got to help me!"

Beyond the cross, Bo was still down, a pitiful sight as he vainly tried to drag himself along, stretching an imploring arm toward Bill Ike. Jake wanted to lay down cover fire, but just as he raised his carbine over the boulder, a bullet pinged and rock exploded almost in his face. He tried a second time, a third, but shards whizzed past his ear whenever he popped his head up.

"I'm pinned down!" he yelled. Then he looked up in desperation at the bouldered slope. "Nub! Need some help! Nub!"

Strangely, it was the first time Jake could remember ever addressing Nub by name, one more regret for a man with a tally book full of regrets. But Nub didn't answer. Maybe he couldn't answer. Maybe he was already as dead as all of them would be in moments.

Still, Jake continued to call, just as Bo kept up his frantic plea.

"Bill Ike! You got to help me!"

Why the snipers hadn't finished off the

young man, Jake had no idea, but when Bill Ike shouted "I'm a-comin', boy!" and rushed into the open, it was clear. First Ruthie had served as bait, and now it was Bo who did.

Not ten feet into the line of fire, Bill Ike dropped to a rifle shot.

"Papa!" screamed Bo. "Papa!"

Sprawled facedown, Bill Ike wouldn't give up. Lifting his head, spewing blood on his gray whiskers with every gurgling breath, he dragged himself on toward Bo, cutting the distance between them even as his leg flopped to another slug. Jake had never thought he would have reason to respect Bill Ike, but he admired the way he clawed through a hail of bullets for someone who wasn't even his own.

Reaching Bo, Bill Ike somehow gained his hands and knees and fell across him, shielding the wounded man with his own body. For a few seconds, Bill Ike writhed every time dust flew from his clothes, and then he grew still, his body jerking lifelessly as it absorbed bullets meant for Bo.

Jake called out again for Nub, his echoing voice interrupted by more gunfire. When there was still no answer, Jake's fragile hopes sank even more. Bo was alive but helpless, and Nub had to be as dead as Bill

Ike. Not only that, but at any moment, a stray slug would find Ruthie, and the shooters would move in and fire a bullet with Jake's name on it. It was sure to happen, and there wasn't a damned thing he could do about it.

He twisted around again, prone and desperate before the gunsight-like notch in the rocks at the drop-off. To scramble over the edge would be suicide, for he found a sheer cliff below, a hundred-foot drop to eternity. Suddenly something caught his eye down and away in the open floodplain, three figures framed in the V of the rocks as they neared the brush along the river.

Dru! God A'mighty, Dru!

It was Dru, all right, but a *bandido* had her in his grip, dragging her at the heels of the taller Mexican whom Jake knew to be Rentería. Man or devil, he was down there, the perpetrator of all this, half-hidden by Dru and his accomplice. In moments the three would be in the brush and gone, and when the shooters on the rim swooped down for the kill, Jake would die knowing that he had left Dru to an end even more terrible than his sister's.

Swiftly he brought up his Marlin and rested the muzzle in the notch. He braced the butt plate against his shoulder and positioned his fingers inside the lever port. Placing his cheek against the wood stock, he looked down the eighteen-and-a-half-inch barrel and found the three of them in the rear and front sights. He wanted to take out the tall figure, but there wasn't a clear shot and he had time enough to fire only once.

This was the moment for which Jake had longed, a third chance to right a forty-seven-year-old wrong even at the greatest of prices. Dru would die and so would he, but hers would be a compassionate death that his own would spare him from mourning.

Taking a bead on the dark hair bouncing between her shoulders, he began squeezing the trigger.

At the last instant, almost against his will, Jake slid the sights a fraction to the side, and with a roar a .44 Special slug exploded from the muzzle at twelve hundred feet per second. The bandit beside Dru crumpled to the ground, startling her and inducing Rentería to whirl. Quicker than Jake ever had before, he levered in another cartridge, but by then it was too late. Rentería had seized his daughter and the two had disappeared into the brush.

Stunned, Jake released his grip on the carbine. Leaving the barrel propped in the notch, he rolled lifelessly onto his back and laid a forearm across his eyes. He could see the terror in Dru's face, the terror in his sister's face. He could see both girls suffering to the bitter end, enduring things unimaginable, all because he hadn't found the courage.

What have I done? Damn me to hell, what have I done?

Jake moved his arm aside, and the gold-hued cross rose up before him, its transverse beam blazed against the blue of the sky. It loomed over him just as his mother had in that moment when he had dropped before her and wept the news of his sister's death. She had drawn him to her breast and spoken to him, the fervent pleas of a loving woman. Now, somehow, this cross also spoke to him, in a way nothing ever had before, with a kind of love he had never dreamed possible. Submitting, a man finally putting aside everything else after all these years, Jake whispered back, asking that he be lifted up.

Boom!

Boom! Boom!

From the vicinity of the dark boulders high on the summit, the reports echoed down, three blasts of a shotgun. Jake seized his carbine and looked up at the section of rim visible from his place of defense. He scouted and tensed and waited — three seconds, five, ten — and when there was no answering gunfire, he knew. Still, he protected himself behind a rock.

"Nub!" he called. "Nub! Nub!"

He thought he shouted over someone's reply, and he went silent and heard it again.

"All is clear, Mr. Graves! All is clear!"

Scrambling to his feet, Jake found the arm of the cross underscoring Nub and the black boulders at the rim. "Rentería's got Dru by the river!" Jake yelled.

He dug out his pocketknife as he rushed to Ruthie. With a quick slice she was free, and a moment later he had the gag out of her mouth.

"They hurt you, darlin'? The bastards hurt you?"

"Bo, Uncle Jake!" she exclaimed as he helped her up. "Is he —"

Jake didn't know as he turned to him, but Bo's arm was stretched out and his fingers were moving. If Jake had questioned whether Ruthie could really love someone like Bo Capps, the way she cried his name as they ran to him dispelled any doubts.

The moment they reached Bo, Ruthie knelt and squeezed his hand, while Jake took Bill Ike's bullet-riddled body by the shoulders and rolled it to the side. Bo was free and very much alive, and he sat up weeping in Ruthie's embrace and repeatedly spoke not only her name, but one long ago forbidden by Bill Ike.

"Papa told me, Ruthie," he said, emotion choking his voice as he placed a hand on Bill Ike's chest. "His life for mine. Papa told me — Papa told me — I wouldn't believe him, but Papa told me, his life for mine."

"You got a gift," said Jake, tearing open a bloody spot in Bo's trouser leg. Then he looked up at Ruthie, who gently brushed the hair out of Bo's eyes. "*Two* gifts. Make the most of 'em."

Jake found only a flesh wound in Bo's thigh, a spot below the hip merely creased by a bullet. It had been pain and a drunkard's panic, not incapacity, that had felled Bo and had kept him down, but maybe Ruthie's love and support could get him back on his feet in the way that mattered most.

Standing, Jake spun to the brushy floodplain, knowing what he had to do.

"Take care of each other!"

Praying he wasn't too late — truly *praying* — Jake bolted in search of a way down.

CHAPTER 20

The swarm of the dead met Jesús Rentería in the place where his sister's blood had run.

They crowded the small clearing, dark forms swaying against the tall cane and screwbeans. They rose up out of the profaned sand and huddled under the black willow's drooping limbs. From saltbush and mesquites, they studied him, ghosts from his past baring their torment.

Trembling at the clearing's edge, Rentería felt the brush of a barbed catclaw as Consuela-who-wasn't-Consuela resisted his hold on her arm.

"Why are you fighting me, Consuela?" he asked. "Have I not brought you back?"

But the devil twin continued to struggle, even here among all the other figures from beyond the grave.

"You left Ruthie to die!" she charged.

"No, no, no, *mi hermana.* I only baited the trap for wolves that would keep us from this place." He swept an arm before them. "*Mira,* see how it looks the same? This cat-claw, *uña de gato,* remember? I dig down and the stain will still be there."

"Stain?"

"Your . . . Your blood, my sister, the place you came up out of *infierno.* Maybe you go back now?"

But the devil twin only stared at Rentería, and his greatest fear seemed very near.

"Or maybe . . ." Rentería was hesitant even to ask. "Maybe you take me to hell with you? *Por favor,* Consuela, please tell me!"

But her lips said nothing, even as her haunting eyes stayed fixed on him.

Again, he motioned to the clearing. "See the faces? See how they met you here? The *niños* and *señoritas* and *viejos,* the dead like you who gave me the blood — all of you are here, watching and waiting. But for what, Consuela? Tell me!"

Her reply was quick and certain. "To see you die! My people are coming for me!"

The devil twin seemed startled to realize that she had said it, for she blanched and tried again to pull away.

"No, *mi hermana! Por favor,* don't say that, my sister!"

"I'm not your sister!"

Now it was Rentería who drew back a little. "Not — ?"

"I'm Drucilla Graves. You carried us off. I'm not Consuela!"

Not Consuela, not Consuela! Every *fantasma* in the clearing seemed to take up the chant and shout it at Rentería. *Not Consuela, not Consuela!* They came closer, reaching out for him with cold hands smeared with their own blood. *Not Consuela, not Consuela!*

Maybe Rentería the *tlahuelpuchi* had gone too long without feeding adequately. Maybe because of it he saw and heard things that weren't there. Maybe the dead all around were just nightmares arising from a need for the blood of the young.

Consuela or not, the *señorita* in his grasp offered sustenance that Rentería could no longer deny himself.

From a worn scabbard at his hip, he withdrew a bone-handled knife — the identical blade with which he had killed Consuela at this very catclaw. The sensations of twenty years past strangely merged with the here and now: the rustle of the catclaw's gray-green leaves, the hanging reek of his sweat, the salty trickle across his lips, the twist of his feet in the sand as he grappled with her.

Whatever she was — sister or *señorita* or she-devil — she fought like the hellion who had lashed his men with a quirt at the Cross C's. She wrestled with him over the knife with a determination that surprised him, but it was a clash that he had always won, and he would win it now.

The ground began to shake under Rentería.

It rumbled and groaned and threw him off balance, a temblor coming in waves, each stronger than the last. He felt a stirring at his boots, and a strange light abruptly shot up between the she-devil and him, a fiery ray that went past the uppermost limbs of the catclaw and disappeared in the sky. He stumbled aside, dragging her with him, and the ground where they had stood seemed to break apart. *Sí,* the earth itself was opening, giving way to a rising figure in a black shroud, and suddenly she stood before him.

Consuela. The fourteen-year-old Consuela. The only Consuela, buried for twenty years.

Her eyes were white and cold and bewitching, the eyes of someone more than dead, and they held him in their spell as her throat dripped where he had once severed the jugular.

"¡*Qué quieres conmigo,* Consuela!" he cried. "What do you want with me?"

With hollow voice, she told him what he already seemed to know.

"By your own hand, Jesús," she whispered. "The way you killed *me.*"

Still, Rentería had to ask. "What do you mean, my sister? Tell me!"

"Die, *tlahuelpuchi.* Die."

From the screwbeans on the near side of the clearing and the black willow across it, from a time as recent as three days and as distant as twenty years, the dead who had given Rentería life took up the chant, demanding their justice.

By your own hand, Jesús.

By your own hand — die, tlahuelpuchi!

Rentería released his captive and sank to his knees in the very spot where Consuela's blood had run. Bringing his knife to his throat, he felt the cold steel as he drew it across his jugular.

And then he felt nothing at all.

Pushing with abandon past devil weed and cholla, Jake broke through a final stand of tall cane and found a thrashing Rentería bleeding out at Dru's feet.

"Dad!"

Dru bolted for him out of the backdrop of

a gray-green catclaw, a far better sight to Jake than a loved one down the barrel of a rifle poised to kill. Nevertheless, he had his carbine ready at his hip and swung the muzzle left and right, checking the black willow and screwbeans and mesquites that bordered a clearing otherwise empty.

"They more of 'em?" he yelled.

"Back on the rim, there's —"

"They's took care of."

"Ruthie's up there! They —"

"She's good. Bo Capps is with her."

He lowered the carbine and opened his arms, eager to accept her, but just as afraid to find out what he had to know.

"They hurt you any?" he asked. "Did the sons a —"

She fell into his arms, and nothing had ever felt so good, stretching all the way back to a time when he had been sixteen.

"They never touched us, Dad. Neither of us." She withdrew enough so that he could see her face, and there was worry in it. "Is . . . Is Nub . . ."

"Headed this way, I expect. Never could've did this without him. Proud to have him with me. Even prouder he thinks so much of you."

Still on edge, Jake whirled when he heard brush cracking behind him, but he relaxed when he saw the tall cane part and Nub emerge a step ahead of Alfonso.

"Dru! Oh, Lord, Dru!"

With Nub's cry, emotion overcame Dru, and as she sobbed Nub's name, Jake stepped aside — only now, after the cross, able to accept this Indian's embrace of his daughter for the blessing it was. Once they were in each other's arms, she showed every sign of never letting him go, and Nub seemed equally set on obliging, for he kept his arms securely around her as he repeatedly whispered "Oh, Lord! Oh, Lord!"

Finally Nub looked over Dru's shoulder, and Jake followed his gaze to Rentería's still body beside the catclaw.

"What's happened here?" Nub asked. He turned to Jake. "Rentería — what's happened, Mr. Graves?"

Dru disengaged from Nub just far enough to draw his attention. "He went to talking to himself. He was trying to kill me, but he started talking to himself and cut his own throat."

Already, Alfonso was approaching the bloody scene, the machete in his hand glinting as he twisted it. The day before, Alfonso had described what he must do with Rentería facedown in the dirt and the sun bright in the machete. But now things had changed.

"Killed hisself, son," Jake told him. "Means he ain't comin' back, don't it?"

"*Sí,*" Alfonso acknowledged, stopping above Rentería's body.

"Time you let it go," Jake added.

"*Sí, Señor* Jake. Like you say to me. Like your mother say to you."

Alfonso dropped the blessed machete of a *tlahuelpuchi* hunter in the bloody pool. For a few seconds he bowed his head, and Jake could only imagine the *muchacho's* emotions before he looked up again.

"My sister, my *mamá,* my *papá,* it over for them now," Alfonso said quietly. "And it over for me."

"Dad?" spoke up Dru.

Turning, Jake listened.

"Tell Nub what you just told me."

Jake smiled for the first time in a long, long while. "We got a long ride ahead. I expect we all got a lot to tell."

But Jake said all there was to say when he stretched out his hand and met Nub's halfway.

changed.

"Killed hisself, son," Jake told him.

"Means he ain't comin' back, don't it?"

"Sí," Alfonso acknowledged, stopping above Renteria's body.

"Time you let it go," Jake added.

"Sí, Señor Jake. Like you say to me, Like your mother say to you."

Alfonso dropped the blessed machete of a Itaixajuani hunter in the bloody pool. For a few seconds he bowed his head, and Jake could only imagine the muchacho's emotions before he looked up again.

"My sister, my mama, my papa, it over for them now," Alfonso said quietly. "And it over for me."

"Dad?" spoke up Dru.

Turning, Jake listened.

"Tell Nub what you just told me."

Jake smiled for the first time in a long, long while. "We got a long ride ahead. I expect we all got a lot to tell."

But Jake said all there was to say when he stretched out his hand and met Nub's halfway.

AUTHOR'S NOTE

This novel is based in part on the Brite Ranch Raid of December 25, 1917, when forty to forty-five riders attacked Brite Ranch headquarters south of Valentine, Texas, and killed three men. I also drew upon the Mexican legend of the *tlahuelpuchi,* a shape-shifting agent of evil who needs human blood to survive. Although all characters are fictitious, I have held largely to the facts of the raid and to *tlahuelpuchi* accounts arising in Mexico, particularly in the state of Tlaxcala. My most important sources were:

Brite Ranch Raid
Weatherby, Lela, tape-recorded speech, location not specified, circa late 1960s, digital version in Nita Stewart Haley Memorial Library, Midland, Texas. Fifteen at the time of the raid, she arrived at Brite Ranch headquarters during the siege and witnessed

many of the events.

Neill, Adaline (identified as Mrs. Van Neill), letter published in "Frontier Christmas Days Re-enacted When Bandits Attack Brite Ranch House," *El Paso* [Texas] *Morning Times,* 28 December 1917. The wife of Brite Ranch foreman T. T. "Van" Neill, she was present at headquarters during the entirety of the raid and related graphic details.

Neill, Sam H., testimony before a U.S. Senate subcommittee, 5 February 1920, in *Investigation of Mexican Affairs,* Sen. Doc. 285, 66th Cong., 2nd sess., Vol 1. Present throughout the raid, Neill provided a detailed account.

Webb, Grover, testimony before a U.S. Senate subcommittee, 5 February 1920, in *Investigation of Mexican Affairs.* Serving in the U.S Army Corps of Intelligence Police, Webb was a guide for U.S. Army troops that arrived at Brite Ranch headquarters shortly after the bandits had fled toward Mexico.

Dowe, O. C., testimony before a U.S. Senate subcommittee, 6 February 1920, in *Investigation of Mexican Affairs.* A U.S. Customs mounted inspector, Dowe arrived at Brite Ranch headquarters soon after the raid and accompanied U.S. Army troops into Mexico in pursuit of the bandits.

Matlack, Capt. Leonard, 8th Cavalry, U.S. Army, testimony before a U.S. Senate subcommittee, 7 February 1920, in *Investigation of Mexican Affairs.* Stationed along the U.S.-Mexico border, Matlack learned details of the raid from three bandits who had participated.

"Many Mexican Bandits Killed by U.S. Troops After a Raid," *El Paso* [Texas] *Herald,* 26 December 1917.

"Troops Kill Ten More Bandits in Fight on the Mexican Side," *El Paso Herald,* 27 December 1917.

"Troops Cross Border in Pursuit of Bandits," *El Paso Morning Times,* 27 December 1917.

"Mexican Bandits Raid Ranch Near Marfa Last Night," *El Paso Morning Times,* 27 December 1917.

"Mexican Bandits Murder Stage Driver and Mexican Passengers at Candelaria," *El Paso Morning Times,* 27 December 1917.

"Langhorne Denies Hun Plot in Mexican Raid," *El Paso Morning Times,* 28 December 1917.

"Mexican Troops Now Pursuing Bandits," *El Paso Herald,* 28 December 1917.

"Mexicans Chase Bandits-Garcia," *El Paso Herald,* 28 December 1917.

"Man Killed Is Ernesto Juarez," *El Paso Herald,* 29 December 1917.

"Boy Ready to Repel Bandits," *El Paso Herald,* 29 December 1917.

"Fears Father Killed, But Hears Man Was Capt. Avila," *El Paso Herald,* 31 December 1917.

"Dead by Sam Neill in Fight at Brite Ranch," *El Paso Morning Times,* 5 January 1918.

Keith, Noel L., *The Brites of Capote* (Fort Worth: The Texas Christian University Press, 1961, originally published 1950).

Tlahuelpuchi

Bitto, Robert, "The Vampire Witches of Central Mexico," Mexico Unexplained (website), (http://mexicounexplained.com/vampire-witches-central-mexico, accessed 2018).

Gonzalez, Roberto Martinez, "The *Nahualli-tlahuipuchtli* in the Nahuatl World," *Journal of the Society of Americanists* [Online], 92-1 and 2, 2006, Online January 15, 2012, (http://journals.openedition.org/jsa/3127, accessed 17 March 2019).

"Vampires in Mexico," Infectious Bite: Revenant Blog (website), (http://infectiousbite.blogspot.com/2009/07/vampires-in-mexico.html, accessed 2018).

Nutini, Hugo and John Roberts, *Blood-sucking Witchcraft: An Epistemological Study of Anthropomorphic Supernaturalism in Rural Tlaxcala* (Tucson and London: University of Arizona Press, 1993).

ABOUT THE AUTHOR

The author of twenty-five books, **Patrick Dearen** is a former award-winning reporter for two West Texas daily newspapers. As a nonfiction writer, Dearen has produced books such as *A Cowboy of the Pecos; Saddling Up Anyway: The Dangerous Lives of Old-Time Cowboys;* and *Castle Gap and the Pecos Frontier, Revisited.* His research has led to fifteen novels, including *The Big Drift,* winner of the Spur Award of Western Writers of America. His other western-themed novels include *When Cowboys Die* (a Spur Award finalist); *The Illegal Man; To Hell or the Pecos; Perseverance; Apache Lament;* and *Dead Man's Boot,* which received the Elmer Kelton Award from the Academy of Western Artists.

A ragtime pianist and wilderness enthusiast, Dearen lives with his wife in Texas.

The employees of Thorndike Press hope you have enjoyed this Large Print book. All our Thorndike, Wheeler, and Kennebec Large Print titles are designed for easy reading, and all our books are made to last. Other Thorndike Press Large Print books are available at your library, through selected bookstores, or directly from us.

For information about titles, please call:
    (800) 223-1244

or visit our Web site at:
    http://gale.cengage.com/thorndike

To share your comments, please write:
    Publisher
    Thorndike Press
    10 Water St., Suite 310
    Waterville, ME 04901